Dead Boys Walking

To my friend Charita.
Peace Love Always !!!

Colone

Dead Boys Walking

Causes, effects and solutions to racial profiling, bullying, drive-by shootings, gangs, and child soldiers.

General Davis and Kofi Quaye

To order additional copies of this book, contact:
Xlibris Corporation
1-888-795-4274
www.Xlibris.com
Orders@Xlibris.com
106159

CONTENTS

DEDICATION

This book is dedicated to all the youth and young adults in this country and around the globe who have lost their lives to violence in the streets, wars, or in other circumstances beyond their control. It is also dedicated to the memories of all the celebrated cases of violence related tragedies namely Trayvon Martin, Troy Davis, Stanley 'Tookie' Williams, and others such as Abu Jamal who have been victimized by the criminal justice system as well as all those we don't know about, not reported or forgotten.

PRESIDENT BARACK OBAMA ON THE TRAYVON MARTIN TRAGEDY

"I have to be careful about my statements to make sure we're not impairing any investigation that's taking place right now. But this is obviously a tragedy. I can only imagine what these parents are going through . . . And when I think about this boy, I think about my own kids. And I think every parent in America should be able to understand why it is absolutely imperative that we investigate every impact of this and that everybody pulls together-federal, state, and local—to figure out how exactly this tragedy happened. I think all of us have to do some soul searching to figure out how does something like this happen. And that means that examine the laws and the context for what happened as well as the specifics of the incident. But my main message is to the parents of Trayvon Martin. If I had a son, he'll look like Trayvon Martin. And I think they are right to expect that all of us as Americans are going to take this with the seriousness it deserves, and that we are going to get to the bottom of exactly what happened."

President Barack Obama

ACKNOWLEDGEMENT

General Davis wishes to take this opportunity to acknowledge the fact that many people and organizations have played significant roles in his life at various points. In as much he would have liked to acknowledge everyone, space limitations make it possible to list the following: my mother, Genell Davis, who is the true example of what love means, [We love you forever, mamma] Pastor Nebraski Carter-Living Waters Church of God In Christ, Imam Hassan—Masjid Abdullah, Julius Edwards of the Dunbar Center, Minister Mark Muhammad—Nation of Islam, Carol and Renee Perry, Lawrence Williams—Syracuse City School Mentoring Program, Walter Eiland, 100 Black Men of Syracuse, Jesse Dowdell-Southwest Community Center, Walter Dixie-Jubilee Homes, Roy Neal-Cuse Connections, Pastor Kenneth Reed, Pastor Jonathan Stevens, Pastor G. Maxwell Jones-Apostolic Church of Jesus Christ, Pastor Phil Turner—Bethany Baptist Church, Rev. Kevin Agee, Carmelita Sapp-Walker, Sam Roberts, Ed Mitchell, James 'Puttin' Jackson, Timothy 'Noble' Jennings, Qasim Salaam, [we miss you, bro] Dr. Karl Newton, Pastor Kevin Stephens, Pastor Pastilla-COGIC-Willie Clayton-[teacher],Joe Lamier-vice principal, Armond 'Skip' Scipione—US Attorney's Office, Al Waymon, Arthur 'Bob' Harrison, Eddie 'Bang Bang' Beuford, Larry Martin-Syracuse University, Ken Kinsey, John Ivory, Gary Morris of G&R Real Estate, Al Gucci—Probation Commissioner, Calvin Marang-Personal Advisor, Amatullah Yamini-HUD and First Lady at Masjid Abdullah, Derrick Carr-Political Coordinator, Local 1099, Bettie Graham-Determination Center of CNY, Judge Langston McKinney, Van Robinson—President, Syracuse Common Council, Bea Gonzalez of Syracuse University, Sean Herring-CEO, Black Expo, Arthur 'Fido' Huddleston, Derrick Dixie-CEO-Dixie Public Relations & Death Road Presentations, Kofi

Annan, Helen Hudson-Mothers Against Youth Violence-Syracuse based youth non violence advocacy group, NAACP, Craig 'Sime' Davis-7 Styles Market, Dan Lowengrad-former Supt. of Syracuse Schools, [thanks for giving me a chance], John McCullough—New Justice Services, Inc., Syracuse School District, Boys and Girls Club of America, Chief Frank Fowler,—Syracuse Police Dept. Big Brothers and Sisters Inc., Sharon Pearson—Creative Impact Inc., Venita of Atlanta, Rev. Al Sharpton of National Action Network, Ramzi Aziz, CEO-Wireless Cell Phone, Charles Garland—Garland Brothers Funeral Home, Dr. Rick Wright, Syracuse # 1 DJ, George Kilpatrick, WCNY, Jackie Robinson-TV3 News, Roger Torence, Rick Torence, Hart Seeley-Post Standard Newspaper, Steven Muhammad-]NYC], Bill Simmons, Syracuse Housing Authority, [my children] Quinnika, Genisha, Genell, Asia, Khadijah, Curleese, Neijayah, Rashad, General Jr., Khalif, Khalil, Khalid, Centerion, General 111, General 4th, General 5th, Derrick-[deceased]

Kofi Quaye acknowledges the following: Dave Prater, William 'Bill' Dewey, Mike Atkins, Nate 'Dogg' Holloway, Jenny Penningston, Eugene 'Trey' Cotten, Tashame Ali and Fulaniyira, Cathren Raines, Ayesha Quaye, Ali Muhammad, Mary Nelson, Brenda Jones, John DeGrassa and Daniel DeGrace, Lawrence Davis.

This is too serious a subject to limit it to the personal and life experiences of one person as initially envisaged when we embarked on this book a few years ago. We had planned it as an expose on the gang life seen through the eyes of an ex gang leader. But it soon dawned on us that limiting it to the personal experiences of an ex-gang leader will not be enough. Youth related violence is just too huge an issue. That's why we decided to make a concerted effort to include data from both government and non-governmental agencies to clarify certain points relative to gangs and youth violence in this country and the world. If credit and acknowledgement are not formally given to sources, it is because we obtained the information and data from research sources such as the Internet where such information or data is presumed to be in the public domain, unless otherwise stated.

It is also an undertaking by two individuals from varying and widely different backgrounds who made the decision to use their knowledge and abilities to put together a book that educates, informs and enlightens the public on youth violence, a subject that impacts or has the potential to affect the lives of most people in one form or another.

We respect, honor and recognize the roles played by various organizations and particularly individuals, living or deceased, whose lives have been impacted by youth violence and who have been mentioned in this book as part of the discussion on the issue of youth violence in Syracuse and elsewhere. The intent is not to exploit the name or reputation of any organization or individual whose name is mentioned. If we mentioned names, it is because they were involved in youth related incidents reported in the media or the roles they played or continue to play were significant and contribute to our understanding of the issue of youth violence.

INTRODUCTION

SYRACUSE, MODEL CITY FOR THE YOUTH

Is Syracuse a model city for the youth of this country and the world? Why not? Syracuse has been an exemplar city in many ways. In the sixties and seventies, it was widely acknowledged as a model city in the United States. It was noted for a number of attributes that made it unique, not the least of which was the role it played as a 'working man's town' in the words of Dave Prater, a long standing resident of the city. As far as we are concerned, that role remains and for the purposes of this book, Syracuse has been elevated to another level in the pantheon of great cities of America; it is a model city for the youth of USA.

On what basis do we make such a lofty claim?

The record of the city of Syracuse speaks for itself. This city has made great strides in its efforts to create conditions that make it possible for its youth and young adults to grow to become responsible citizens who accomplish great feats. A wide variety of programs have been put in place, designed to provide the youth and young adults with the proper environment and incentives to stay in school, finish high school and pursue higher education. Programs such as the SAY YES TO EDUCATION have made significant contributions to the attainment of those goals and have gained national and global recognition for their innovative and pragmatic approach to the education of youth and young adults

In sports, Syracuse reigns supreme as the city that has given the world many of its greatest athletes. The history of Syracuse points out that the youth and young adults of this city have been outstanding athletes in all fields. Many legendary sports figures of today and yesteryear had their beginning right here in this city. These include Jim Brown, Ernie Davis, Dave Bing, Derrick Coleman, Art Monk, Carmelo Anthony and many of the legendary sports figures whose accomplishments continue to inspire the athletes of today. It continues with the outstanding performances of the Syracuse University football and basketball teams.

That feat has been replicated in all areas of life. Simply stated, Syracuse is a city that has produced generations of youth and young adults who have excelled in sports, business, industry, academia, and the sciences and arts.

Elsewhere in this book we have also stated that the co-authors of this book, Kofi Quaye and General Davis are long term residents of the city of Syracuse. General Davis was born and raised in Syracuse, while Kofi Quaye became a resident several decades ago. Our collaboration on this book is significant in many ways, it is the first time, at least to our knowledge, that an African-American and an African have teamed up to write a book about gangs and youth violence in the United States.

That Syracuse becomes the focus of this book is not a coincidence. It reflects one reality; the authors know the city of Syracuse.

WHAT THIS BOOK WILL DO FOR THE YOUTH AND YOUNG ADULTS AND CITY OF SYRACUSE

The need for this book is beyond question. Youth violence has been as huge a problem in Syracuse as it has been in cities of similar size and constitution all over the country, perhaps more so as a result of the unique circumstances that make Syracuse what it is: the main city in Central New York. Our goal is to increase awareness of the problem of youth violence as part of the overall effort to curb and ultimately stop youth violence. As alluded to above, the city of Syracuse has made every effort to reduce the incidence of youth violence. Politicians, leaders of business and industry, governmental and non-governmental organizations and ordinary citizens have contributed to the effort in significant ways. So serious is the problem of youth violence taken in this city that in November 2011, Helen Hudson, an advocate of stop youth violence movement and an African-American was elected to the Syracuse Common Council.

The timing for the publication of this book couldn't have been better. Youth violence is in the news constantly. And the root causes are often attributed to gangs. The media in Central New York, led by the Post Standard continue to focus on youth violence, seeking ways and means to curb and stop it altogether. To be sure, Syracuse has had its share of problems with the youth and young adults and we don't claim to have all the answers. This book discusses youth violence and explores strategies that can help in creating more awareness about the magnitude of the problem. We also aspire to create, build and sustain a gang prevention center in Syracuse that will focus most of its programs and activities on what we discuss in this book and plan to do with funds generated from the sale of this book, or donations from anyone who wishes to help with such a project.

We love the city of Syracuse and want our youth and young adults to stop becoming victims of youth violence and live long and positive lives as law abiding citizens. That can happen if youth violence stops or becomes less of a problem.

We salute all those who have made Syracuse proud in their youth. These include Khalid Bey, the youngest African-American to be elected to the Syracuse Common Council, Helen Hudson, Alfonso Davis and all the young men and women involved in programs and activities that benefit the youth and young adults. We also salute Syracuse University basketball coach, Jim Boeheim, Sports Director, Darryl Gross, and all the athletes who have made significant contributions to preparing and nurturing the talents of our youth and young adults as they transitioned from young adulthood into the world of professional sports. They have all made Syracuse proud by the contribution they have made to making it a leader in college and professional sports.

One objective will be accomplished by this book, regardless of what happens in the wake of its publication; it puts the city of Syracuse in the midst of the on-going debate on youth violence in this country and around the world.

HOW TO USE THIS BOOK

This book discusses youth violence in all its manifestations and breaks it down in simple terms, and most importantly from the perspective of people who have literally 'done it, been there and know all about it' from first hand experience and can discuss it with authority.

General Davis is not necessarily proud of the fact that his claim to fame may lay more in his role as an ex gang leader than anything else. By the same token, his background and experiences in the streets have provided him with the depth of knowledge, insight and perspective to be able to discuss youth violence and make suggestions with respect to what can be done to alleviate or completely eradicate it.

Years of living in the inner city and writing about the African-American experience gave the co-author, Kofi Quaye, the chance to gain a deep insight into life in the urban setting that forms the core of the Syracuse African-American community. He has been associated with and cultivated close associations with men and women who helped him to navigate the rather murky and sometimes dangerous terrain of the underworld of the African-American community and emerged with a considerable degree of understanding that makes it possible for him to write about youth violence. He has known kids like Dante who came from a one parent home, who worked with him as a preteen with delivering the local Pennysaver, and who got caught up in the criminal life as a teenager, ended up doing various terms in the prison system and had two kids before he turned twenty. Donte's partner [he had gravitated towards the gay lifestyle in his early twenties], a transgender, was shot at close range and killed by another young adult in what came to be described as the first hate crime to be prosecuted by the State of New York. He has known and was mentored by a former law enforcement officer, David Prater, from whom he learned about law and order as it relates to the African-American community. Mike Atkins also played a key role in his understanding, enlightenment and awareness of the dynamics of life in the African-American community.

Just weeks before we went to print, a series of shootings took place on the south and west sides of the city of Syracuse. They were nothing new to people who live in those areas. Similar incidents have occurred in the neighborhood before and had become known as volatile areas, prone to acts of violence. Problem was; it had begun far too early this year. What will happen during the long summer days ahead? Then came news of the tragedy of Trayvon Martin, the seventeen year old African-American shot to death in Sanford, Florida and all hell broke loose.

PRELUDE

WHAT DOES 'DEAD BOYS WALKING' MEAN?

There is no question about the fact that the title of this book will prompt many to ask what we mean by 'dead boys walking'.

Why precisely does it mean? The answer is simple. It refers to an entire generation of young African-Americans, and by implication, young men and women of other races whose lives are in danger as a result of the circumstances in which they find themselves, whether by accident or design. Specifically, it refers to young African-American men and women, all over the country and the globe who may not live too long as well as those who have lost their lives as a result of violence.

And these include men and women such as myself, General Davis of Syracuse, the co-author of this book who happens to be alive today only because I was lucky to have survived. That is about the only way I can explain why I am alive today to write about my experiences. How else can I describe it considering the fact that I was targeted to be killed several times, shot at close range on several occasions, and was ambushed many times by others with the intention of killing me? That is what we are talking about when we refer to 'dead boys walking'. I was a typical 'dead boy walking'. The kind of lifestyle I led as a gang leader had set me up to deal with violence and the potential of an early, premature death on a daily basis.

We, and this includes most of my contemporaries and our peers, were all dead boys walking in the context we are talking about, and didn't even know it. Everything we did brought us close to death. Death stalked us, loomed above us, and hovered around us in every move we made. And we were totally clueless. In this regard, we cite the case of Stanley

'Tookie' Williams, the infamous gang leader from Los Angeles who was executed for crimes he was alleged to have committed as a leader of the Crips gang. He was a prime example of a 'dead boy walking'. The kind of life he led and his death constitute a classic case of a man who fits precisely what we are talking about when we refer to a 'dead man walking'. In his case, tragically as in most, he paid the ultimate price; he died a violent and premature death, though not directly as a victim of street violence. He was executed by the state of California.

Many have been ensnared in the 'dead boys walking' trap and don't even know it. And they are all over the place. We are talking about youth and young adults who have set themselves up to be killed, either by the police, a rival gang member or by someone with a weapon, crazy enough and ready to use it when they find themselves being robbed, attacked or otherwise placed in a situation where they have to defend themselves. The recent tragedy that befell Trayvon Martin definitely made him a 'dead boy walking'

Some of us have survived, and are alive and kicking today, but the harsh, brutal truth is this: our lives were in danger for the longest. And still may be in danger. We are talking about men and women of my age who led the thug life or thought they did and paid for it by doing time in prison, became addicted to drugs and alcohol, picked up other bad habits and have not been able to change their lives around, no matter how hard they tried. The drugs, the stress of prison life, the strain of trying to be a step ahead of the law take its toll, making men like myself hardened, street smart, but still vulnerable to acts of violence perpetrated by others with whom we were beefing or had other issues with. We were prone to being gunned down, knifed or otherwise targeted for violence; we were unwitting or willing participants in activities that could lead to premature death. We were 'dead boys walking'

Sadly, that applies to most of the youth of today. The youth of today, particularly those from the African-American community are nothing short of an endangered species. It is scary when you think about it. Everything we did back in the day and continue to do now pushes, edges us closer to death. It can be about saying the wrong thing to the wrong person or looking at the wrong person the wrong way. Anything can set off a chain reaction that can get someone shot, knifed or beaten to death. It is a jungle out there. It is so dangerous a territory that those who know what the deal is, watch every step they take, every word they say and every move they make.

Again, many of us were lucky to have survived. Others didn't and ended up dead. A few just hang in there, hooked and addicted to drugs and alcohol, leading the thug life, knowing that any minute the streets would catch up with them and they'll either have to shoot and kill someone or be shot and killed themselves

The kids of today in America find themselves in pretty much the same situation. The media publish stories of young men and women whose lives are cut short in acts of violence. No matter where you live, whether in a little town in Middle America or in an urbanized setting such as New York, from big cities in the Northeast to the Deep South, the youth and young adults face dangerous times and live in a world where violence co-exists with everything else, as it did back in the day when we were growing up.

As already pointed out above, we were all 'dead boys walking' and didn't even know it. Worse yet, those who didn't get killed in shoot outs didn't escape the victimization process altogether. We are messed up by our experiences in the streets and haunted by a past from which we cannot redeem ourselves, regardless of what we do to try to erase the past.

A few emerged from the streets stronger and wiser with a deeper insight and knowledge about the world, the neighborhoods, people and life as a whole. As a result, they seem to be better prepared to deal with life, at any level. They learned to not only survive, but thrive in the worst circumstances. Among those who have written books about the streets and have become successful authors and motivational speakers, and getting paid to write and speak about their experiences are men such as Nathan McCall, the author of MAKES ME WANNA HOLLER. His book has become a seminal work on life for young African-American men in America today, especially when it comes to dealing with incarceration and the criminal life in general.

Some have emerged as leaders, taking on causes that allow them to use their knowledge of the streets to help others save themselves from becoming victims and from continuing to be 'dead boys walking'.

But before we get into the problem of youth violence from the personal standpoint, which will be personal experiences of young men and women who have been impacted by youth violence, we need to break it down in terms of what it means when we talk about it in the context of this book.

CHAPTER ONE

WHAT FORMS YOUTH VIOLENCE TAKES: CASES THAT DEMONSTRATE THE PREVALENCE OF YOUTH VIOLENCE IN AMERICA IN BOTH SMALL AND LARGE COMMUNITIES

In as much as acts of violence committed by the youth and young adults can and do happen in both small and large communities the world over, we'll begin by focusing on the incidence of youth violence and its impact on a city we know quite well. By that we are referring to the fact that the authors of this book know the city of Syracuse, if only by virtue of the fact that we both live and work in this city, and have seen immense changes take place over the years. Most importantly, we have been a part of this community and have been impacted, like everyone else, by everything that has happened during that period. These span the spectrum from politics to sports to race relations to economic development to education and culture. In the political arena, we have seen the emergence of a number of powerful African-American politicians culminating with an African-American becoming the president of the City Common Council. In sports, we have witnessed the consistently outstanding performances of the Syracuse University football, basketball and lacrosse teams. Similar feats of excellence have been replicated in all facets of life in this city with the youth and young adults playing a key role.

Syracuse is by all accounts a quintessential medium sized American city. Often referred to as the major city in Central New York, it was once a thriving industrial city, but has been impacted in many ways by the recent economic downturn. Like most cities in the United States, it had to endure hard times as a result of the changes in industry and business and the overall unstable national economy in recent years. As a result, mainly from the economic downturn, many of its industries closed or moved out of town. Unemployment and joblessness have been major issues and the city has lost a considerable portion of its population and is now faced with a future full of challenges, not unlike other cities in America.

One challenge it has had to deal with in the past is youth related violence. And it has been a problem of major proportions. Youth related violence became so serious a problem that it appeared to threaten to overshadow the other more positive attributes of the city, especially with the kind of media hype it created.

The following incidents of youth violence will provide some insight into the gravity of the problem. They were culled from newspaper reports published in the Post Standard, the major newspaper in Central New York. These acts of violence took place within a relatively short period of time and project a picture of a city with a serious problem of youth criminal behavior, some of them resulting in the premature death of the victims.

Twenty three year old Sudanese immigrant, Ahmed Mohammed was found dead in an empty apartment building on the Southside of Syracuse. Police found enough evidence to conclude he had died from wounds inflicted by gun shots. More than a decade later, his murder remains a mystery.

Travis Robinson was shot sitting in his mother's van. Monique Meeks was shot talking to his friends. Sammy Perry was shot walking out of a store. Henry Sullivan was shot standing outside a bar on State Street.

Mel went out with his friends to a night club at Armory Square in downtown Syracuse. At some point during the night, he decided to step out for a moment. That was the last time his friends saw him alive. He was gunned down in the parking lot.

Latiesha 'Momo' Cannon and his brother sat in a car on the west side of Syracuse, waiting to go to a party in a house in the neighborhood. Suddenly, shots rang out. Someone had sneaked up on them, pointed a gun and shot into the car. Momo was hit. It was fatal.

A twenty month old baby, yes, a twenty month old baby was hit by a bullet in a van late 2010. A teenage boy was out in a neighborhood street, with a number of other teenagers, going from door to door, asking for candy as kids usually do on that one Halloween night in an age old tradition called trick and treat.

Suddenly, shots rang out. The kids ran for cover, but it was too late for one of them; he was hit and had to be rushed to the hospital, where he was treated.

As alluded to above, all these acts of violence happened in Syracuse in Central New York and were reported by the local newspaper, the Post Standard and most of the television and radio stations in the city.

The list reads like hits by gangsters in Mafia style shootings and killings. The victims were gunned down and left to die. And most did not survive. Many died instantly on the spot. Others died in the hospital after being rushed there or on the way to the hospital.

Many of the murders have been solved. Some are still being investigated. A few have just gone cold. In the cold cases, police tell parents, family members and other interested parties that the investigations have not been completely forgotten or abandoned, only not actively being pursued, as a result of either slow or no progress. They cite lack of evidence as reasons for the slow pace of progress in finding those responsible for the murders.

A number of factors stand out as you read the grisly list of cold blooded murders. The majority of the victims were young, mostly in their late teens. And they were mostly African-Americans. Again, what makes their murders more remarkable is the fact that they all took place in Syracuse, in upstate New York.

No wonder the media hype that followed in the wake of the shootings was intense. The series of shootings and murders proved to be too much for the general population of the city. The media did a good job at covering the shootings, providing details of the murders, all of which gave readers and the people of Syracuse reason to continue to ask and speculate openly if the city's law enforcement had lost control or just couldn't deal with the situation.

Not surprisingly, the idea of a city the size of Syracuse lacking the capacity or unable to stop youth violence made the residents of the city very nervous. The question that was raised by all the media was; why? Why would a city of the size of Syracuse, fall victim to such a crime wave? So far these questions remain unanswered.

The current chief of police of the Syracuse Police Department, Frank Fowler is an African-American and has made several statements in the past relating to the issue of youth violence. He is as concerned as everyone about the rising incidence of youth violence in the city of Syracuse and would like to see an end to the problem, he has said.

Problem is: youth violence has not been completely eliminated. It continues to be an issue and most parents and youth and young adults feel just as unsafe as they were a few years ago when it seemed as though law enforcement had lost its capacity to control youth violence in the city of Syracuse.

CHAPTER TWO

WHAT IS YOUTH VIOLENCE AND WHY IS SO MUCH ATTENTION BEING PAID TO IT?

Let us begin with a definition of youth violence and try to figure out what it is all about and why there is so much hype about it today. What precisely do we mean when we talk about youth violence?

What is often referred to as youth violence are acts of violence in which youth and young adults are involved. It is mostly committed against the youth and young adults and committed by the youth.

Youth violence happens everywhere and can happen to anyone regardless of their race, social status, economic and financial standing. No matter where you live, how you live and where you go, youth violence is one thing that cannot be totally excluded from your life. More so, if there are young ones in the family.

Teen violence causes, incidence, and risk factors

Homicide is described as the second leading cause of death among young people ages 10 to 24. Research by experts have revealed that in this age group, it is the leading cause of death for African-Americans, the second leading cause of death for Hispanics, and the third leading cause of death for American Indians, Alaskan Natives, and Asian Pacific Islanders These were the findings of experts who investigated the subject of youth violence for years.

Figures released by both government and non-governmental agencies confirm the fact that homicide is the leading cause among young people ages 10-24. According to the Center of Disease Control,

[CDC] in 2001, the year for the research study on the subject of youth violence, 5,486 young people ages 10 to 24 were murdered, an average of 15 each day [CDC]

The same data pointed out that in 2001, 79% of homicide victims ages 10 to 24 were killed with firearms. In a related nationwide survey that investigated the factors that contributed to the upsurge of youth violence in the early two thousands. It was noted that 17% of students reported carrying a weapon. These weapons included guns, knifes, and clubs.

Among students nationwide, it was also noted that 33% reported being in a physical fight one or more times in the preceding 12 months. Nationwide, 9% of students reported being hit, slapped, or physically hurt on purpose by their boyfriend or girlfriend in the 12 month period.

The above data represents statistical data compiled by government agencies and non-governmental organizations in an attempt to come to grips with the problem of youth violence in its various manifestations. The figures reveal one important fact; it shows that it is a big problem that poses real danger not only to the lives of the youth and young adults: society as a whole is impacted. Simply stated, it is as bad as it can get; it is real and possibly won't be easy to reverse any time soon and has to be dealt with. By the same token, it shouldn't be taken as an impossible situation or that nothing can be done about it. As a matter of fact, a lot is being done about it by the leadership of cities, counties and states across the country as well as governmental and non-governmental organizations-NGO'S—and individuals and their efforts have paid off. We'll deal with that in another chapter.

CHAPTER THREE

GROUPS AT RISK OF YOUTH VIOLENCE

As alluded to in the previous chapter, youth violence has become a very serious problem in contemporary American society. Data collected by government, non-governmental and law enforcement agencies shows the seriousness of the problem. It has emerged as one of the most pressing issues facing the nation today and a subject often discussed in the media. Media hype, both print and electronic, about youth violence has hit an all time high and continues to increase in intensity. And the focus is on curbing or stopping youth related violence.

Youth violence has also become one of the hottest issues for people seeking office in all parts of the country. No politician seeking office can avoid discussing it if they consider themselves as serious candidates with an agenda that will get them elected to office. They have to deal with it and have to provide answers outlining what they intend to do about the problem of youth violence when campaigning for votes. Otherwise they run the risk of turning off neighborhood residents and voters who have problems with or view youth violence as an issue.

To get an idea of the seriousness of the problem of youth violence, we'll focus on data for the year 2001. It was reported that of the 5,486 homicides in the 10 to 24 age group in 2001, 85% (4,659) were males and 15% (827) were females (CDC 2004).

A nationwide survey found male students (41%) more likely to have been involved in a physical fight than female students (25%) in the 12 months preceding the survey. A nationwide survey found female students (12%) more likely than male students (6%) to have been forced to have sexual intercourse

The above paints a pretty dismal picture when it comes to the issue of youth related violence in the United States. Overall, the conclusion that can be drawn from the data is simply this: it is an unsafe world out there for the youth and young adults. No matter how you look at it, that's just what it is. So the question remains: what can be done to protect the youth and young adults of today?

Families have been known to take extraordinary measures to protect their young ones from falling under the influence of outside forces, only to find out later that their efforts have been in vain. Those with the resources make sure their children go to exclusive schools, and interact with others from the same background, etc. In spite of all the precautionary measures, those measures don't protect the young ones from the dangers that lurk in the streets.

There is no question about the fact that the problem of youth violence has moved to center stage in the national consciousness. And the point to note is this; youth violence has increased in regularity and intensity. Available evidence, provided and reinforced to some degree by the above statistics and data, suggests that it has been on the rise the past several years and appears to show no sign of slowing down.

Efforts to find solutions have been initiated all over the country and around the globe. Law enforcement agencies, non-profit organizations, city, county, state and federal agencies as well as individuals have committed themselves to finding solutions. Problem is; they haven't succeeded in stopping the rising incidence of youth violence. If anything, it seems to be increasing in the United States and around the globe. Child soldiers are one major issue we have to deal with in today's world.

In other countries around the world, youth violence has become a major problem. In Africa, in particular, youth violence manifests itself in ways that have shocked the world. We are talking about youth and young adults playing a key role in wars, forced to kill each other and operating in total lawlessness as a result of the circumstances in which they find themselves. We'll discuss it in detail in another chapter.

CHAPTER FOUR

DIFFERENT FORMS OF INSTITUTIONALIZED YOUTH VIOLENCE

Youth violence occurs in many different forms. More often than not, it has as its main arena, the streets. That is where most of the action takes place. We are talking about gang fights, turf battles, territorial conflicts, drive by shootings, revenge and retaliatory attacks. They all take place in the streets and are often the main causes of youth violence.

The words 'Let's take it to the streets' are often used when the youth and young adults decide to seek judgment on their own, through their own devices and in an arena where most parents and law enforcement can do nothing about: the streets. It means the argument or confrontation is being taken to another level where violence is the final arbiter.

On the other hand, there are other forms of youth violence that occur indoors, often in plain sight of adults that end up with many sustaining serious injuries, psychic and physical. These are what we would refer to as institutionalized forms of youth violence. One such form of institutionalized form of youth violence is bullying.

Bullying

Bullying has been described as a common experience for many children and adolescents. Surveys indicate that as many as half of all children are bullied at some point during their school years, and at least 10% are bullied on a regular basis.

Bullying behavior can be physical or verbal. Boys tend to use physical intimidation or threats, regardless of the gender of their victims. Bullying by girls is more often verbal, usually with another girl as the target. Bullying has even been reported in online chat rooms, through e-mail and on social networking sites.

Children who are bullied experience real suffering that can interfere with their social and emotional development, as well as their school performance. Some victims of bullying have even attempted suicide rather than continue to endure such harassment and punishment.

Children and adolescents who bully thrive on controlling or dominating others. They have often been the victims of physical abuse or bullying themselves. Bullies may also be depressed, angry or upset about events at school or at home. Children targeted by bullies also tend to fit a particular profile. Bullies often choose children who are passive, easily intimidated, or have few friends. Victims may also be smaller or younger, and have a harder time defending themselves.

If you suspect your child is bullying others, it's important to seek help for him or her as soon as possible. Without intervention, bullying can lead to serious academic, social, emotional and legal difficulties. Talk to your child's pediatrician, teacher, principal, school counselor, or family physician. If the bullying continues, a comprehensive evaluation by a child and adolescent psychiatrist or other mental health professional should be arranged. The evaluation can help you and your child understand what is causing the bullying, and help you develop a plan to stop the destructive behavior.

If you suspect your child may be the victim of bullying, ask him or her to tell you what's going on. You can help by providing lots of opportunities to talk with you in an open and honest way.

It's also important to respond in a positive and accepting manner. Let your child know it's not his or her fault, and that he or she did the right thing by telling you. Other specific suggestions include the following:

- Ask your child what he or she thinks should be done. What's already been tried? What worked and what didn't?
- Seek help from your child's teacher or the school guidance counselor. Most bullying occurs on playgrounds, in lunchrooms, and bathrooms, on school buses or in unsupervised halls. Ask the school administrators to find out about programs other schools and communities have used to help combat bullying,

such as peer mediation, conflict resolution, anger management training, and increased adult supervision.
- Don't encourage your child to fight back. Instead, suggest that he or she try walking away to avoid the bully, or that they seek help from a teacher, coach, or other adult. The problem with this approach may be that the youth or young adult who seeks help from the authorities be it a teacher, the police or a counselor runs the risk of being called a punk. Worse yet, they may be labeled as a snitch if they ask for help and that is the worse reputation anyone can have in the world of the young and restless. It's the most uncool thing to do. And so in a way you are damned if you do and damned if you don't.
- Help your child practice what to say to the bully so he or she will be prepared the next time.
- Help your child practice being assertive. The simple act of insisting that the bully leave him or her alone may have a surprising effect. Explain to your child that the bully's true goal is to get a response.
- Encourage your child to be with friends when traveling back and forth from school, during shopping trips, or on other outings. Bullies are less likely to pick on a child in a group.

According to experts, there are signs to look for in your child that will indicate problems with bullying. They are all too obvious and can be detected by any parent. All you have to do is to be vigilant and keep your eyes open. If your child becomes withdrawn, depressed or reluctant to go to school, or if you see a decline in school performance, additional consultation or intervention may be required. A child and adolescent psychiatrist or other mental health professional can help your child and family and the school develop a strategy to deal with the bullying. Seeking professional assistance as suggested earlier can lessen the risk of lasting emotional consequences for your child.

Child Soldiers

The 'dead boys walking' syndrome has manifested itself in different parts of the world and has impacted the lives of young people in ways that have sent shock waves around the world. We are talking about child soldiers, an issue that has been widely discussed in the global media. If any particular group of young people can be described as 'dead boys walking' none is more fitting than child soldiers. These are young kids, both males and females, forced to become professional killers at an early age, coerced into becoming part of war machines that carry out missions with the goal of maiming and killing people.

The problem of child soldiers is most critical in Africa, where children as young as nine have been involved in armed conflicts. Children are also used as soldiers in various Asian countries and in parts of Latin America, Europe and the Middle East.

The majority of the world's child soldiers are involved in a variety of armed political groups. These include government-backed paramilitary groups, militias and self-defense units operating in many conflict zones. Others include armed groups opposed to central government rule, groups composed of ethnic, religious and other minorities and clan-based or factional groups fighting governments and each other to defend territory and resources.

Most child soldiers are aged between 14 and 18. While many enlist "voluntarily" research shows that such adolescents see few alternatives to involvement in armed conflict. Some enlist as a means of survival in war-torn regions after family, social and economic structures collapse or after seeing family members tortured or killed by government forces or armed groups. Others join up because of poverty and lack of work or educational opportunities. Many girls have reported enlisting to escape domestic servitude, violence and sexual abuse.

Forcible abductions, sometimes of large numbers of children, continue to occur in some countries. Children as young as nine have been abducted and used in combat. A number of initiatives designed to help in the demobilization, disarmament and reintegration of youth and young adults called (DDR) programs and specifically aimed at child soldiers have been established in many countries, both during and after armed conflict and have assisted former child soldiers to acquire new skills and return to their communities. However, the programs lack funds and adequate resources. Sustained long-term investment is needed if they are to be effective.

Despite growing recognition of girls' involvement in armed conflict, girls are often deliberately or inadvertently excluded from DDR programs. Girl soldiers are frequently subjected to rape and other forms of sexual violence as well as being involved in combat and other roles. In some cases they are stigmatized by their home communities when they return. It has been suggested that programs should be sensitively constructed and designed to respond to the needs of girl soldiers.

Children are forcibly recruited into armed groups in many conflicts but the vast majority of child soldiers are adolescents between the age of 14 and 18 who "volunteer" to join up. However, research has shown that a number of factors may be involved in making the decision to actually join an armed conflict and in reality many such adolescents see few alternatives to enlisting. War itself is a major determinant. Economic, social, community and family structures are frequently ravaged by armed conflict and joining the ranks of the fighters is often the only means of survival. Many youths have reported that desire to avenge the killing of relatives or other violence arising from war is an important motive.

Poverty and lack of access to educational or work opportunities are additional factors—with joining up often holding out either the promise or the reality of an income or a means of getting one. Coupled with this may be a desire for power, status or social recognition. Family and peer pressure to join up for ideological or political reasons or to honor family tradition may also be motivating factors. Girl soldiers have reported joining up to escape domestic servitude or forced marriage or get away from domestic violence, exploitation and abuse.

CHAPTER FIVE

FACTS ABOUT YOUTH VIOLENCE

Gangs

Gang violence has been defined as mostly illegal and non political acts of violence perpetrated by gangs against innocent people, property, or other gangs. And it's nothing new; it has been around for a long time, according to historians. Throughout history, such acts have been committed by gangs at all levels of organization. Nearly every major city was ravaged by gang violence at some point in its history. Modern gangs introduced new acts of violence, which may also function as a rite of passage for new gang members.

For instance, it has been reported that 58 percent of L.A.'s murders were gang-related in the year 2006. Reports of gang-related homicides are concentrated mostly in the largest cities in the United States, where there are long-standing and persistent gang problems and a greater number of documented gang members, most of whom are identified by law enforcement. But the impact of gangs is just as deadly no matter where it occurs, regardless of where it occurs; it has been known to disrupt lives in rural communities as well as in urban settings.

Motives

Usually, gangs have gained the most control in poorer, urban communities and the Third World in response to unemployment and other services. Social disorganization, the disintegration of societal institutions such as family, school, and the public safety networks enable groups of peers to form gangs. According to surveys conducted internationally by the World Bank for their World Development Report 2011, by far the most common reason people suggest as a motive for joining gangs is unemployment.

Ethnic solidarity is also a common factor in gangs. Black and Hispanic gangs formed during the 1960s in the United States often adapted nationalist rhetoric. Both majority and minority races in society have established gangs in the name of identity. The Igbo gang Bakassi Boys in Nigeria defend the majority Igbo group violently and through terror, and in the United States, whites who feel threatened by minority rights have formed their own groups, such as the Ku Klux Klan. Responding to an increasing Black and Hispanic migration, a white gang called Gaylords formed in Chicago.

Most gang members have identifying characteristics unique to their specific clique or gang. The Bloods, for instance, wear red bandanas, the Crips blue, allowing these gangs to "represent" their affiliation. Any disrespect of a gang member's color by an unaffiliated individual is grounds for violent retaliation, often by multiple members of the offended gang. Tattoos are also common identifiers, such as an '18' above the eyebrow to identify an 18th Street (gang) member. Tattoos help a gang member gain respect within their group, and mark them as members for life. They can be burned on as well as inked. Some gangs make use of more than one identifier, like the Nortenos, who wear red bandanas and have '14,' 'XIV,' 'x4,' and 'Norte' tattoos.

Gangs often establish distinctive, characteristic identifiers including graffiti tags, colors, hand signals, clothing (for example, the gangsta rap-type hoodies), jewelry, hair styles, fingernails, slogans, signs (such as the noose and the burning cross as the symbols of the Klan] flags, secret greetings, slurs or code words and other group-specific symbols associated with the gang's common beliefs, rituals, and mythologies to define and differentiate themselves from rival groups and gangs.

As an alternative language, hand-signals, symbols, and slurs in speech, graffiti, print, music, or other mediums communicate specific informational cues used to threaten, disparage, taunt, harass, intimidate, alarm, influence, or exact specific responses including obedience, submission, fear, or terror. One study focused on terrorism and symbols states that symbolism is important because it plays a part in impelling the terrorist to act and then in defining the targets of their actions. Displaying a gang sign, such as the noose, as a symbolic act can be construed as a threat to commit violence communicated with the intent to terrorize another, to cause evacuation of a building, or to cause serious public inconvenience, in reckless disregard of the risk of causing such terror or inconvenience . . . an offense against property or involving danger to another person that may include but is not limited to recklessly endangering another person, harassment, stalking, ethnic intimidation, and criminal mischief.

The Internet is one of the most significant mediums used by gangs to communicate in terms of the size of the audience they can reach with minimal effort and reduced risk. The Internet provides a forum for recruitment activities, typically provoking rival gangs through derogatory postings, and to glorify their gang and themselves. Gangs are using the Internet to communicate with each other, facilitate criminal activity, spread their message and culture around the nation. As Internet pages like MySpace, YouTube, Twitter, AIM, and Facebook become more popular, law enforcement works to understand how to conduct investigations related to gang activity in an online environment. In most cases the police can and will get the information they need. However, this requires police officers and federal agents to make formal legal requests for information in a timely manner, which typically requires a search warrant or subpoena to compel the service providers to supply the needed information. A grand jury subpoena or administrative subpoena, court order, search warrant for user consent is needed to get this information pursuant to the Electronic Communication Privacy Act, Title 18 U.S.C. 2701, et seq. (ECPA). Just about every gang member has a personal web page or some type of social networking internet account or chat room where they post photos and videos and talk openly about their gang exploits. The majority of the service providers that gang members use are free social networking sites that allow users to create their own profile pages, which can include lists of their favorite musicians, books and movies, photos of themselves and friends, and links to related web pages. Many of these services also permit users to send and receive private messages and talk in private chat rooms. Many times a police officer may stumble upon one of these pages, or an informant can get you into the local gang page, providing you a name and password to use to get in and explore. Other times you do not have that option and will have to formally request the needed information. Most service providers have four basic types of information about its users that may be relevant to a criminal investigation; 1) basic identity/

subscriber information supplied by the user in creating the account; 2) IP log-in information; 3) files stored in a user's profile (such as "about me" information or lists of friends); and 4) user sent and received message content. It is important to know the law, and understand what exactly we can get service providers to do and what their capabilities are. It is also important to understand how gang members use the Internet and how we can use their desire to be recognized and respected in their sub-culture against them.

Incarceration

Arrest rates of young people for homicide and other violent crimes skyrocketed from the early eighties to the mid nineties. In response to the dramatic increase in the number of murders committed by young people, Congress and many state legislatures passed new gun control laws, established boot camps, and began waiving children as young as 10 out of the juvenile justice system and into adult criminal courts. Then, starting in the mid-1990s, overall arrest rates began to decline, returning by 1999 to rates only slightly higher than those in 1983.

Several important indicators were used to track youth violence during these years, but their findings did not always agree. Arrest rates, as noted above, provide strong evidence of both a violence epidemic between 1983 and 1993/1994 and a subsequent decline to 1999. Several other indicators of violence furnish similar, but not as robust evidence of a violence epidemic that later subsided.

A rise and subsequent decline in the use of firearms and other weapons by young people provides one potential explanation for the different trends in arrest records and self-reports. The violence epidemic was accompanied by an increase in weapons carrying and use. During this era, instant access to weapons, especially firearms, often turned an angry encounter into a seriously violent or lethal one, which, in turn, drew attention from the police in the form of an arrest. As weapons carrying declined, so did arrest rates, perhaps because the violence was less injurious or lethal. But the amount of underlying violent behavior (on the basis of self-reports) did not change much. If anything, it appears to have increased in recent years. That undercurrent of violent behavior could reignite into a new epidemic if weapons carrying rises again. From a public health perspective, a resurgence of weapons carrying—and hence the potential for another epidemic of violence—poses a grave threat.

Arrests for Violent Crimes

The Federal Bureau of Investigation (FBI) monitors arrests made by law enforcement agencies across the United States through the Uniform Crime Reporting (UCR) program. Since the 1930s, this program has compiled annual arrest information submitted voluntarily by thousands of city, county, and state police agencies. This information currently comes from police jurisdictions that represent only 68 percent of the population, so FBI figures represent projections of these data to the entire U.S. population.

Significant work has been undertaken by individual researches in areas such as the role played by firearms in the increasing incidence of youth violence and they have been cited for providing considerable insight into the study and analysis of youth violence as a result. The work of two researchers appears to have had considerable impact over the years. It is the team of Snyder and Sickmund.

The Uniform Crime Reporting program tabulates the number, rate, and certain features of arrests made by law enforcement agencies. Because some people are arrested more than once a year, the UCR cannot provide an accurate count of the number of people arrested or the proportion of the total population arrested. Nor can the UCR provide an accurate count of the number of crimes committed. A single arrest may account for a series of crimes, or a single crime may involve the arrest of more than one person. Young people tend to commit crimes in groups, so the number of youths arrested inflates the number of crimes committed

As noted earlier, arrest rates are also prone to certain types of error. Unless indicated otherwise, the figures on arrests were assembled by the FBI.

From the data provided by the federal law enforcement authorities and findings attributed to individual researchers as noted above, it has been suggested that the easy availability of guns and the resulting rise in lethal violence was caused at least in part by the emerging crack cocaine markets in the mid-1980s and the recruitment of youths into these markets, where carrying guns became routine. It also resulted from changes in the types of guns manufactured, with cheaper, larger caliber guns flooding the gun markets

Arrest Rates and Trends

Statistics complied by government agencies indicate that overall arrest rates for violent crimes by youths between the ages of 10 and 17 rose sharply from 1983 to 1993/1994. Rates then declined until 1999, the most recent year for which figures are available.

According to research findings published In 1999 by social scientist Snyder, arrests of young people for all crimes totaled 2.4 million with 104,000 arrests for violent crimes. Arrests for aggravated assault (69,600) and robbery (28,000) were the most frequent, with arrests for forcible rape (5,000) and murder (1,400) trailing significantly behind. In 1998, youths accounted for one out of six arrests for all violent crimes, a share that has decreased slightly (16 percent) in recent years Although the 1999 arrest rate for violent crimes was the lowest in that decade, it is still 15 percent higher than the 1983 rate. The 1999 rates for homicide, robbery, and rape are below the 1983 rates; however, arrests for aggravated assault are still nearly 70 percent higher than 1983 rates.

The sheer magnitude of the increase in arrest rates between 1983 and 1993/1994 is striking. Overall, arrest rates of youths for violent offenses grew by about 70 percent. The increase in homicides committed by young people was particularly alarming. Both the rate of homicide arrests and the actual number of young people who were arrested for a homicide nearly tripled. This increase was consistent for adolescents at each age between 14 and 17

The Role of Firearms

The decade-long upsurge in homicides was tied to an increased use of firearms in the commission of crimes. Likewise, the downward trend in homicide arrests from 1993 to 1999 can be traced largely to a decline in firearm usage. The critical role of firearms in homicide and other violent crimes is supported by arrest, victimization, hospitalization, and self-report data.

Analysis of arrest data shows an unequivocal upsurge in firearm usage by young people who committed homicide. In 1983, youths were equally likely to use firearms and other weapons, such as a knife or club, to kill someone. By 1994, 82 percent of homicides by young people were committed with firearms. Virtually all of the increase in firearm-related homicides involved African American youths The precipitous drop in homicides between 1994 and 1998 coincided with a decline in firearm usage, again mostly by African American youths.

Homicides Commited by the Youth Against Other Youth

From July 1, 2004 through June 30, 2005, there were 48 school-associated deaths in elementary and secondary schools in the United States. (Indicators of School Crime and Safety: 2006, U.S. Departments of Education and Justice, 2006) Incidents of crime were reported at 96 percent of high schools, 94 percent of middle schools, and 74 percent of primary schools. (Crime, Violence, Discipline and Safety in U.S. Public Schools: Findings from the School Survey on Crime and Safety: 2003-04, National Center for Education Statistics, 2006)

Six and one half percent of students surveyed reported that they had carried a weapon on school property within the last thirty days, while 18 percent said they carried a weapon anywhere during the past month. (2005 Youth Risk Behavior Survey Results, Center for Disease Control, 2006)

Six percent of students had not gone to school on one or more of the 30 days preceding the survey because they felt they would be unsafe at school or on their way to or from school. (2005 Youth Risk Behavior Survey Results, Center for Disease Control, 2006)

The percentage of public schools experiencing one or more violent incidents increased between the 1999-2000 and 2003-04 school years, from 71 to 81 percent. (Indicators of School Crime and Safety: 2006, U.S. Departments of Education and Justice, 2006)

Youth surveyed for the annual Uhlich Report Card graded adults for the following questions: 30.5% graded a C for protecting kids and teens from gun violence 30.3% graded a B and 30.2% graded a C for keeping schools safe from violence and crime 32.7% graded a C for getting rid of gangs (The Uhlich Report Card: America's Youth Grade Adults, Uhlich Children's Home of Chicago, 2004)

CHAPTER SIX

VICTIIMS OF YOUTH VIOLENCE

We will now deal with the victims of youth violence. And the question is: who precisely are the victims of youth violence?

The victimization of youth takes many forms. It includes child abuse, child sexual abuse, bullying, gang violence and youth-on-youth attacks, rape and murder. In alarming rates, young people are turning to violence to resolve their problems and to criminal activity as a lifestyle choice.

There are many theories about this type of violence. Some theorists suggest that children learn from their environment—be it the influence of a crime filled neighborhood, an abusive home, or an isolated rural area where support services are minimal.

Regardless of where it happens, youth violence has become a major problem. So huge a problem has it become that it has taken center stage in most communities as one of the most pressing problems to be dealt with.

Victimization

The following data reveals the immensity of the problem of youth violence in the United States. According to figures released by the Center for Disease Control in its 2006 report titled Youth Risk Behavior Survey, nationwide, 29.8 percent of students had their property (e.g., car, clothing, or books) stolen or deliberately damaged on school property one or more times during the twelve months preceding the survey. (2005 Youth Risk Behavior Survey Results, Center for Disease Control, 2006)

In 2005, four percent of students ages 12-18 reported being victimized at school during the past six months. Approximately three percent reported theft, one percent reported violent victimization, and less than half of a percent reported serious violent victimization. (Indicators of School Crime and Safety: 2006, U.S. Departments of Education and Justice, 2006)

The percentage of students who were threatened or injured with a weapon has fluctuated between 7 to 9 percent in all survey years from 1993 through 2005. (Indicators of School Crime and Safety: 2006, U.S. Departments of Education and Justice, 2006)

Students' likelihood of being threatened or injured with a weapon on school property was examined by race/ethnicity. In 2003, American Indian students (22%) were more likely than Black (11%), Hispanic (9%), and White (8%) students to report being threatened or injured with a weapon on school property. (Indicators of School Crime and Safety: 2005, U.S. Departments of Education and Justice, 2005)

In 2003-04, 10 percent of teachers in central city schools were threatened with injury by students, compared with 6 percent of teachers in urban fringe schools and 5 percent of teachers in rural schools. Five percent of teachers in central city schools were attacked by students, compared with 3 percent of teachers in urban fringe and 2 percent of teachers in rural schools. (Indicators of School Crime and Safety: 2006, U.S. Departments of Education and Justice, 2006)

Communities across America are responding by offering a multitude of programs to help decrease youth crime and victimization. Parenting skills development programs have been established in many communities to educate parents about coping skills and positive anger management, in hopes of reducing child abuse and domestic violence in the home environment.

In addition, school systems are beginning to develop intervention programs aimed at detecting child abuse. Such programs are integrated within school systems and offer children and youth a safe haven to turn to when a crisis occurs. Educators have stressed the importance of developing educational curricula which teach self-esteem, conflict resolution skills, respect for cultural diversity and pride in one's culture.

Effective curricula in this area are introduced in early childhood education and are consistently reinforced throughout the duration of a child's education. Such efforts require the support of parents, teachers, social workers and community leaders working together.

How effective has been your city's efforts to deal with the problem of youth related violence? Most cities in America and indeed the world, have in place programs and activities geared towards advocating for and on behalf of the youth, aimed at making the world safe for the youth and young adults. It remains to be seen how effective these efforts have proven to be.

Reference is made above to the role that certain factors can play in making that happen. These include but are not limited to programs focusing on helping parents to develop effective parenting skills, the incorporation of intervention programs into school curricula, etc, etc.

You probably have read about these and similar community based initiatives in the city, town or village in which you live. The question remains and is simply this; how successful have these efforts proven to be? The next chapter deals with some of these programs in greater detail.

Culled and complied from data from the Internet.

CHAPTER SEVEN

PROGRAMS DEALING WITH AT RISK YOUTH

One approach that has been used in an attempt to address youth violence is the development of programs where at-risk youth are united with inmates to see first hand, the consequences of anti-social, criminal behavior. The innovative "Impact of Crime on Victims" program sponsored by the California Youth Authority is one such program. It teaches youthful offenders about how their criminal actions affect their victims, their families, their communities, and themselves.

Media reports indicate that the 'impact' program appears to have proven to be effective in the past when it was used as part of the ongoing effort aimed at finding a way to combat youth violence. Basically, it involved exposing youth and young adults to situations they are likely to encounter if they find themselves behind bars. In other words, the inevitable result of engaging in criminal behavior is an arrest that will ultimately lead to jail, either for a long or brief term, depending on the nature of the crime. Regardless, it is an experience that has many myths built into it in ways that seem to make it less threatening to youth and young adults. This program is the only one of its kind that was set up that makes it possible for people outside prison walls to go inside and see what life in jail is all about for inmates. And all indications are life behind bars is nasty, demeaning and dangerous. And the 'impact' project proved to be one of the most effective ways of exposing the realities and horrors of prison life to the youth and young adults

The message is direct, in your face and up-close and personal. The participants actually go through the same motions that inmates go through when they make their initial contact with the penal system. The experience, from those who had gone through it, can be best described as the closest you can get to see what life is like for people behind bars. For the moment; at least the period during which the youth are in the company of inmates, they are as much in confinement, as the actual prisoners are. They are denied their freedom: their every action is monitored. If they fantasized about it, they are actually living it, at that moment. And many have found out that experience horrifying, albeit brief, enough to scare them from doing anything that will get them to go to prison for real

Another approach that has been experimented with is the volunteer opportunities program. It offers volunteer opportunities for youth, neighborhood crime watch and mentor programs. Such programs empower young people to feel a sense of responsibility to their communities and some control over their future.

Programs such as these can begin to address violence against children, an investment that is essential to society's future. Marian Wright Edelman, founder of the Children's Defense Fund, sums up the importance of this goal: "The in attention to our children by our society poses a greater threat to our safety, harmony, and productivity than any external enemy."

Youth and the Internet

Adults are not the only ones spending time online. More than 30 million U.S. children have online access (Pew Internet and American Life, 2001). According to a study by the National Center for Missing and Exploited Children, 1 out 5 youth ages 10-17 who use the Internet regularly received at least one sexual solicitation over the past year (Finkelhor, 2000). More disturbing is that less than 10 percent (10%) of sexual solicitations are reported to authorities such as a law enforcement agency, an internet service provider, or a hotline

Youth can be easy prey for online predators. Parents and care-givers need to monitor the time children spend online. Teaching youth to safeguard personal information is also an effective method of safety planning. Online safety awareness for youth is extremely important.

Arthur 'Fido' Huddleston of Syracuse has made youth non violence a cause to which he has dedicated himself. He has attended several funerals of youth and young adults in the Syracuse area who lost their lives to youth related violence and has collected several obituaries, powerful reminders of the tragedy and loss that can be created by youth violence

me

The Davis Boys and their sister with
their mother, Genell Davis

They were all supposed to be innocent school kids
until they got involved in neighborhood gangs.

General Davis and some of his 'boys' back in the day.

CHAPTER EIGHT

RISK FACTORS FOR TEEN VIOLENCE

On the surface, they sound like profound academic theoretical formulations that can be understood only by people with college degrees or similar educational credentials. To be sure, the uninitiated or those with limited knowledge may be easily intimidated on being confronted with such terminologies.

By the same token, they can be broken down into very easily understandable common denominators. We will break them down to make it easier for readers who may not have the time to do their own research to be able to relate to them.

Individual Factors in Teen Violence:
Attention deficits/hyperactivity

You have heard it umpteen times. The term anti-social behavior is widely used by both professional and non professional people when referring to behavior by people that turns other people off. In other words, it basically means behaving in ways that are not normal, and which as a result makes other people upset and want to stay away from you or gives them a reason to decide to discontinue their association or dealing with you. Teens are just as prone to behaving in a manner that can be described as anti-social and which can get them in trouble with family and friends. Lately, the term ADD has come into currency and is being used to describe the same kind of behavior

History of early aggressive behavior.

This refers to behavior in teens that doesn't fit the norm in terms of intensity and regularity and is done over a long period of time. For instance, any teen who wants to fight all the time or is always picking on other kids fits into this category.

Involvement with drugs, alcohol, or tobacco

It means precisely what it says. Any teen who develops a habit of drinking alcohol, smoking marijuana or 'weed' and cigarettes has already began the descent into a life of bad habits that will lead to health problems in the future and impaired judgment when under the influence. It can also lead them to behave in ways that can get them in trouble. It just sets you up to do illegal stuff in order to be able to keep up with or continue with those habits

Low IQ

Teens with low IQ are those who show obvious signs of inability to think fast and act just as fast in response to normal life situations. In such cases, what seems to pose no problem to normal kids comes across as problematic to them. In effect, they are less able to process information with the same speed like those who have normal IQ

Poor behavioral control

Basically teens who cannot seem to be able to control impulses to engage in bad behavior or do nasty things to others and don't care what or who they hurt in the process.

Social cognitive or information-processing deficits

It basically means the same thing as LOW IQ. Teens with less than normal ability to process information and act accordingly have what is described as social cognitive or information processing deficits.

Early involvement in general offenses

Teens who get in trouble with the law by doing things they are not supposed to do. It simply amounts to breaking the law and being arrested or going to jail as a result.

Family Factors in Youth Violence

The following have been cited as some of the factors in a family setting that contribute to youth violence They include authoritarian childrearing attitudes, exposure to violence and family conflict, harsh, lax, or inconsistent disciplinary practices, lack of involvement in the child's life, low emotional attachment to parents or caregivers, low parental education and income, parental substance abuse and criminality, poor family functioning and poor monitoring and supervision of children

There is more on this in another chapter in which General Davis tells his own story and focuses on almost all the issues raised in this section. He describes growing up in the projects in Syracuse as an experiment in survival for most teens at the time.

Protective Factors for Teen Violence Prevention

Regarding the prevention of youth violence, researchers have also identified a number of contributing factors that play a role in effectively combating youth violence. The Protective Factors include intolerant attitude toward deviance, high IQ, positive social orientation, commitment to school and involvement in social activities

How do you sum up all of the above? It's a breakdown of the variables involved when it comes to dealing with teen violence prevention and the role a family can play in the process. They are the factors that contribute to creating conditions that give rise to youth violence as well as factors that prevent youth violence.

More than likely, they are known by social workers, youth workers and others involved in various aspects of youth work. What we don't know is how effective they have been when applied to different situations in different communities.

CHAPTER NINE

OTHER VICTIMS OF VIOLENCE: PARENTS. FAMILY. FRIENDS. COLLEAGUES. COMMUNITY

Parents of victims of youth violence are impacted in ways that affect them in almost every aspect of their lives. First and foremost is the loss of an offspring. The loss of an offspring is certainly one of the most painful experiences any parent has to go through. It is a loss of great magnitude. And that sense of loss is compounded and made more painful when the cause of the death is youth violence.

Women have played a significant role in making youth violence an issue that cannot be ignored. As a result, they have been thrust into the limelight for taking the initiative in many areas. Many have shown their concern by either talking to the media, or writing about youth violence. Others have become involved in organizations that have dedicated themselves to advocating for and on behalf of the youth. A few have become leaders and have gained local, national and even global recognition for taking up the cause. One such person is Helen Hudson from Syracuse, New York.

She is the president and co-founder of Mothers Against Gun Violence, a Syracuse based organization that advocates for and on behalf of the youth in Syracuse. In media interviews, Helen Hudson has stated that she has always been one to fight for the underdog. "I've always had a mouth," she said. Born outside Jackson, Mississippi, she remembers intense racial conflict. "With my mouth," she reflects, "if I had stayed in Mississippi and had to grow up in that era, I probably wouldn't have made it." She is currently AFL-CIO Community Services Liaison to the United Way of Central New York. In November 2011, she was elected as a Common Councilor at-Large as a Democrat.

According to Helen Hudson, she and her colleagues started the organization around the year 2002, because 'it was the year we had the highest homicides in the City of Syracuse. It bothered me that every day you would wake up and you would hear that someone's child had been murdered in the streets. And there was no outcry. There was not any outrage from the minority community, or from any community. I went to one of the pastors and I asked him if there was a way that we could go out into the streets and do outreach with these young people. He in turn informed me that if I did that, I was setting a bunch of mothers up to get killed. That kind of threw me for a loop, and it set me back, but I went to Rev. Ellis, and that particular night he was having his prayer patrol. He invited me to come down and tell the group what we were doing, trying to start, and why we were doing it. We worked with them that summer."

Since then, she has been actively involved in advocating for youth non violence and has made a huge impact on the entire city of Syracuse as a result of her work on behalf of youth and young adults, particularly in activities and programs geared towards stemming the tide of youth related violence and murders in the city of Syracuse.

As a common councilor, she has been elevated to a position where she can apply the power, influence and prestige of her status as a lawmaker to make things happen for and on behalf of the cause she has dedicated herself; stopping youth related violence and killings in the city were she lives and works.

There are other parents who are not as celebrated as Helen Hudson, but whose lives have been impacted by youth violence; they have figured out ways to deal with the loss and the tragedy of losing their children to violence in the streets.

One such parent is Renee Evans of Syracuse and she continues to deal with problems caused by youth violence. Her son, Mel was shot to death by another young adult. He was in his late teens. She still feels the pain of the loss of her only son.

"He was so young. He had a whole life ahead of him, cut short by another youngster who is now in jail," she said. It was a tragedy for both victim and perpetrator; life in prison for one and the grave for the other.

We alluded to the fact that the streets and the thug life have a way of either destroying the lives of young African-American men or toughening them and contribute to making them get a deeper insight into life. Arthur Huddleston is such an individual who has taken the initiative to do something about youth violence in the city in which he was born and raised. A big guy in terms of physique, the Syracuse native's combination of height and bulk makes him an awesome and menacing presence. It also gave him strength, agility and stamina, all of them lethal attributes that can be used to deadly effect in street fights. Huddleston lived up to his image: he intimidated most of his peers and managed to create a reputation in the streets as a formidable fighter. That was not enough, though, to stop someone from trying to kill him. He was shot three times in the head at close range. Miraculously, he survived. He has since committed himself to advocating for and on behalf of non violence related programs and activities. He has collected a number of obituaries, mostly of young men who suffered premature deaths as a result of youth violence.

Arthur 'Fido' Huddleston believes his involvement in activities and programs geared towards preventing youth violence will ultimately help curb and potentially stop youth violence in Syracuse. The entire community has to get involved and create more awareness of the problem. One thing most parents have do is to talk to talk to their kids to stay in school and do everything they can to keep them in school and encourage them to not get involved in gangs or gang related activities, he says.

CHAPTER TEN

THE YOUTH AND THE STREETS; 'BEEFING', DRUGS, GANGSTA AND THUG LIFESTYLE THE POWER OF THE STREETS

Why do kids prefer to hang out in the streets? Why do the streets appear to have such a powerful and often fatal attraction for the youth and young adults? Why is the gangster or gangsta lifestyle so popular with the youth these days?

The answer is this: the streets in the neighborhoods offer a home away from home for most kids. They prefer to hang out with their friends in the streets rather than stay home and do such things as their home work after school, watch television or read. Most school age kids feel that way about staying at home and do everything they can to get out, even if it means sneaking out without their parent's knowledge and or approval.

One factor that drives them to the streets has been described as not enough attention from single mothers who are stressed out themselves and don't have the presence of mind or the time to pay close attention to their children. Young kids who don't have much going for them at home in terms of parental love, attention and guidance are at risk for a simple reason; they can be easily coerced into doing the wrong things by adults who have no real love for them, who pretend to be caring and compassionate. And many criminal elements use that method to prey on vulnerable youth and young adults.

Being out there in the streets brings them in contact with what's going on. In the streets nonstop action of all kinds takes place, regardless.

Police presence in neighborhoods doesn't stop criminal activity; it just makes the criminals resort to other ways of doing business that the police may not know about, or have a hard time trying to figure out. The vulnerable youth and young adults see the street hustlers doing their illegal business of hustling drugs and driving nice cars and wearing the latest fancy clothes. More than likely, the drug dealer might be the uncle of a friend or a neighbor. Or someone they know in the neighborhood. They begin to see the potential the streets offer to make quick money. Soon he and 'his boys' begin to hang around the street corners, looking for something to do that will bring in fast 'money' or 'loot'. At this point they don't really care what kind of hustle they would get themselves into. All they want to do is 'get the money'. They think they can get away with it just like the others; what they don't know is the real story behind those who seem to be invincible. The hustlers are not as invincible, powerful and slick as they portray themselves. In most instances, they are trying to stay one step ahead of the law. Sooner or later, the law catches up with them and off to jail they go.

Hanging out in the street corner means only one thing; the hustle is on; the street hustle and life has begun. It doesn't take long before they are recruited by older hustlers looking to expand and increase the numbers of young hustlers working for them. It is a street culture that attracts the young and restless in ways too powerful for the impressionable teenagers to resist.

The following chapters focus on what the youth, young adults and their parents can do to fight off the temptation to 'hustle' and get in trouble or get killed as a result.

CHAPTER ELEVEN

THE STREET LIFE AND THE THUG LIFESTYLE

Today the street life is described as the thug life, giving it a totally new meaning. Not too long ago, a thug was nothing more than a common hustler who survived in the streets by committing small time crimes. Lately, that appears to have changed. Now the thug life is part of the culture of the gangsta lifestyle, glamorized to a certain degree by the hip hop culture. Young boys seem to have no shame in referring to themselves, even boasting about being thugs when they are really talking about life in the streets, not the thug life in the conventional definition of the term.

It is what we would describe as the glamorization of the thug life. Suddenly, there is no stigma attached to being a criminal or behaving in criminal ways. It is called 'living large', living beyond their means, regardless of how you do it. If it means selling drugs or robbing people in order to be able to 'maintain' as they say, so be it.

There is no doubt about the fact that the hip-hop culture has played a leading role in the glamorization of the thug life in recent times. The major contributor has been the music. First of all, the language in the music leaves a lot to be desired in terms of how it describes the lifestyles of the people who make that kind of music and the targeted audience, impressionable young men and women who absorb everything they hear, and often think the lyrics are talking about real things in real life.

And mostly, it's all about getting high, sex and quite often, messing with the police. Ordinarily, law abiding kids would not smoke marijuana, or do other drugs, think constantly about sex and look at the police as the enemy. But that's what the lyrics in most of the latest hip-hop songs talk about.

When Snoop Dogg talks about 'rolling down the street, smoking indo, sipping on gin and juice,' he's most certainly referring to drinking out in the open, which is against the law in most cities. Any kid who gets caught drinking in the open, faces prosecution from the law, but if Snoop says it's the cool thing to do, most kids are likely to gravitate towards doing what they hear in the song. It becomes the cool thing to do and break the law as a result. And it's because, among the youth and young adults, no body wants to be seen as the one caught doing the un-cool thing.

They begin hustling, which basically is selling drugs, and it doesn't take long for them to come under the radar screen of the local police who cruise the neighborhoods in undercover cars. They have set themselves up to either go to jail or get killed.

But the street hustle is not all that, so to speak. It is the worst possible career choice any youth or young adult can make. It has no benefits and only guarantees nothing but problems with law enforcement, time in jail and a strong probability of early death as well as making those who choose such a lifestyle candidates for the title of 'a dead boy walking'. And a dead boy walking means precisely what it says; a youth or young adult who is going through the motions of life but whose fate is already decided; he will be shot to death or killed by other methods of violence before his time. It doesn't have to happen that way, but more than likely it will, only because of the lifestyle he will lead.

Not too long ago, the bling became one of the symbols of the thug life. It has all but disappeared for one simple reason; it was a way for law enforcement to identify and arrest or harass suspected drug dealers, pimps and other criminals who thought they could get away with wearing symbols that gave hints of what they were up to.

CHAPTER TWELVE

THE BEGINNING OF THE CRIMINAL LIFE FOR THE YOUNG: HOW THE THUG LIFE OPERATES IN BOTH RURAL AND URBAN AREAS: THE STORY OF THE CORLEONNES GANG IN SYRACUSE

Back in the day, there was a gang in Syracuse. They called themselves the Corleonnes. They ruled the streets; or so it seemed: at least they thought they did, in part because they committed a lot of crimes and didn't get arrested or face prosecution for a long time until things caught up with them and they found themselves looking at doing time in the penitentiary.

We are talking about a number of youth and young adults who decided to call themselves the Corleonnes, after watching the Godfather movie which featured the Mafia family with the same name. They were once described in the local media as the most dangerous gang in Central New York.

They robbed people and thought it was cool. They shot at each other and didn't see anything wrong with it. They lied about almost everything and felt they were justified in doing so. And stayed high off cocaine, 'weed' or marijuana and other drugs, or liquor and believed it was the right thing to do.

In the end, they found out they were wrong with the lifestyle they led. By that time, some of them had been killed; many were behind bars; a few had retreated from the streets. And the police were pressing up on them from every angle, using all kinds of methods: intimidation, trickery; lies, traps, blackmail and unwarranted arrests. Law enforcement deployed all the weapons at their disposal in an effort to stop them.

Many gang members tried to run, and didn't get far before the law caught up with them. Others did time and got out after a long stretch. A few copped pleas and got off with lesser sentences.

But it all comes down to one thing: they were all 'dead boys walking'. in the sense of what we are talking about in this book.

In other words, these were youth and young adults who had the impunity to believe they could commit crimes and get away with it. We are talking about young men and women who described themselves as members of the first real gang in the city of Syracuse; they were the original gangsta. Again, that was what they thought, until they were proven wrong.

Back in the day, members of a gang were called gangsters. Today, it is gangsta, or a gang banger, and other names that have been coined over the years.

The question becomes; were they real gangsters, or just dead boys walking?

They thought they were gangsters, and that was what mattered to them at the time. They could care less what others thought about them. So long as they had the guts to think that way, such it was. So long as they had the clothes, the girls, and the money and could 'live large', the kind of lifestyle made possible as a result of criminal activity, they felt it was perfectly legit to call themselves gangsters.

They felt powerful, but had no real power; just the illusion of it, as a result of what they did and got away with in terms of the criminal life. To make matters worse, they were all young, mostly in their upper teens, but already acting like grown men. Looking back at how things went down, many of them who survived shootouts and jail realize how lucky they are to be alive today. Others didn't make it. They got killed and their names are distant memories today.

According to General Davis, co-author of this book: "I got shot: not once, not twice; quite a few times, and survived. How I managed to survive, after I was ambushed, and shot at close range remains a mystery to this day. The people who came at me had only one thing on their mind; get rid of me. Not that I didn't expect it. I did; just that it happened when I least expected it and it almost did it for me.

Again, I survived seemingly against all odds. I was a 'dead boy walking' and didn't even know it. Apparently, Allah wasn't ready for me. All I can say is I was spared so I could try to help out today's youth and young adults from following in our footsteps."

CHAPTER THIRTEEN

DO ABSENT FATHERS CONTRIBUTE TO VIOLENT TENDENCIES IN YOUTH AND YOUNG ADULTS?

Do absentee fathers and single parent households have anything to do with the high incidence of the criminal or gangster life among the African-American youth and young adults back in the day or today? Are boys and girls raised by single mothers or single fathers, in some instances, more likely to end up in the streets than those raised in two parent homes? How do the streets seem to have that kind of power they have over the youth and young adults turning them from innocent teenagers to dangerous drug dealers, cold blooded killers, hardened criminals, thugs and felons with long criminal records?

The streets are powerful, mean, dangerous and deadly. That is the harsh, brutal reality we all have to live with. The evidence is all too obvious. If the popular media is to be believed, these are the stereotypical notions that hold sway. The drive-by shootings in the streets, the seemingly senseless murders, muggings and other forms of violence that occur in the streets bear testimony to the dangers that lurk in the streets for the youth and young adults. How and why the streets play a key role in shaping the criminal mentality of thugs and criminals have been written about as part of the ongoing effort to analyze the dynamics that make them powerful and irresistible to boys and girls and turn them into criminals.

Again one thing is for sure: the streets have a mystique that even the most hardened criminals and thugs don't understand. It's not all about the typical street scenes we see on television and in movies with kids hanging out in corners with hoodies covering their faces, talking tough, smoking weed and looking mean and packing guns.

It is the streets that hide the young killers who go out to kill other youth for reasons that are often hard to fathom. It is hard to explain what the streets really represent from the standpoint of the power they seem to have and the attraction for the youth and young adults who just want to go out there and kill or engage in behavior that endangers their own lives as well as those of others.

Why do most kids like to hang out in the streets even if they have nothing to do out there? From where do the streets derive their power over the youth and young adults?

It's not easy to answer these questions. All we know is the streets seem to have some kind of a fatal attraction for most kids, particularly from the hood. We know it even as pre-teens that the streets are dangerous in every way you can think of. We know you can get hit by a car or a bicycle if you are not too careful when we are real young, but it doesn't stop even the young ones from riding their bikes in the streets.

Basically, the streets are where the action takes place. If you want to fight someone you take it to the streets. If a boy feels grown and wants to do grown people stuff, you go out in the streets. If you want to show your boys you can hustle or you are cool; If you want to show off your gun, knife, or new sneakers, you go out in the streets. You can go out there and 'kick some ass'. By the same token, you can also get your ass kicked. Worse yet, you can get killed very easily by someone with a gun who won't think twice before pulling the trigger.

The streets provide the youth and young adults with a false sense of security. They learn early that they can hide in plain sight in the streets, and do things they can't do at home. A lot of youth and young adults tend to take to the streets early. Why? Because of the feeling of freedom it gives them. Being out there in the streets gives most kids that sense of freedom they don't have when they are home; not with mama and big brothers and sisters watching every move.

After a while they get tired of watching television or being confined to their rooms or doing what their parents or older siblings tell them to do. They know there is always something going on in the streets and they don't want to miss it. So they think of any lie they can tell, or try to figure out a way to sneak out and join the other kids and hang out.

One thing is for sure. There are certain things you can do and get away if you are dealing only with a mother who has other concerns on her mind. We are not suggesting that mothers are not smart or are not up to speed; it's just the way it is. Boys are wired to be a little faster than girls physically as we all know and they don't stop at trying to exercise their ability to talk fast or get way from their mothers. It's a different story when there is a father or a man around. Fathers or men just seem to know what kids are planning on doing even before they do it and it is because we are wired the same way. That makes a big difference. More than likely, the absence of role models makes it easier for youth and young adults to gravitate towards the criminal life.

The question remains: is there a correlation between the high incidence of youth violence and the well documented rate of absentee fathers in the African-American communities?

We don't have definitive answers to that question. Again, this is one area we defer to experts. We are talking about sociologists and others who have the expertise, knowledge and insight to make a determination regarding the role absentee fathers might have played in the incidence of the inordinately high incidence of youth violence in the African-American community.

Most people know how it feels like to grow up in a home without a father. It is certainly not an ideal situation, if only for the fact that kids need to have both parents around as they grow up. When one is missing for any reason, it creates a problem, as evidenced by the high incidence of youth violence and youth related criminal activities in the African-American community.

CHAPTER THIRTEEN

THE FEAR FACTOR? POLICE AND OTHER LAW ENFORCEMENT TACTICS THAT ENDANGER THE LIVES OF YOUTH AND YOUNG ADULTS

The worst fear of most people living in a predominantly African American neighborhood, if they'll admit it, is for a police car to pull up behind them while they are driving. More than likely, they would be asked to 'pull over'. It almost never fails. All the police need to make that decision to pull you over is to see a young Black person in their late teens to early thirties driving a 'sharp' really nice looking vehicle in any neighborhood. It doesn't really matter whether it is a white, mixed or a predominantly African-American neighborhood, or a poor or rich area. The possibility of being targeted by the police increases if the car happens to be an expensive late model. In most instances, that is all it takes to get stopped by the police in any city, town or village in America, especially, if the driver happens to be young and an African-American.

Most people who live in the 'hood' in most parts of the United States know only too well that all you have to do to set yourself up to be stopped by the police is to be spotted behind a nice 'whip' in any city in the United States. The police in most cities in the United States can turn driving a nice car into a probable cause to stop a young African-American and make an arrest. It has become a recurring subject that has been debated in the media and hyped by the African-American media in particular.

It has been referred to as racial profiling, and discussed extensively in terms of its implications for law enforcement, the administration of criminal justice and race relations as a whole. But nothing much has changed, even though public consciousness of the problem has been raised, it has not stopped.

Again, regardless of who you are, where you are going and what you are doing, the sight of a police car behind the car you are driving in the hood usually spells trouble, and more so if you happen to be a young Black man. More than likely, you'll be pulled over. The police know how to get you or give you a ticket for some kind of violation once they make that decision to stop you. Your driving record may be clean, your driving skills may be perfect, and the car can be brand new with no obvious defects. The cops know just what to do to get you once you're spotted.

But knowing about the possibility of being stopped and harassed by the police doesn't prevent young Black men from driving nice cars. They don't allow that knowledge to intimidate them. They don't see any reason why they should deny themselves the privilege of driving. Instead of instilling fear into the youth and young adults, they develop feelings that are of ambivalence more than anything else, which easily turns into defiance after a while. They simply make the decision to not be intimidated by the police and operate on the assumption, rightly or wrongly, that you can't do right by the police, no matter how hard you try; not when you're an African-American.

The hell with the police is their attitude. We live in a free country. 'I can ride whenever I get ready'. And therein lies the problem. It sets the stage for the fatal confrontations that have become all too common in the streets of America. The police stop a young Black man. He stops and steps out with an attitude. The cop senses the attitude and knows he has the upper hand. By the same token, the cop knows that the young man is capable of anything. He could be carrying a gun, drugs, and wouldn't want to go to jail. Before you know it, the police have him backed up against a wall, or the hood of the car, handcuffed and headed to jail. Or he makes a wrong move; the police open fire; and he is killed.

That is a dead boy walking.

On the other hand, a young white man driving a similar car in a white neighborhood does so without thinking or worrying about anything, certainly not about a police car pulling up behind him. He has no reason to. He is not worried about being pulled over because he's driving a nice late model car. When he sees a police car pull up behind him, he's glad to know that the police are in the vicinity doing their job. He feels safe; he feels protected; he has no reason to feel otherwise.

One sad example was what happened to a Syracuse native, in another city. Syracuse native Johnny Gamage was shot and killed by Pittsburgh police a few years ago. His crime; driving a Jaguar in a nice neighborhood in Pittsburgh. He was in his early twenties and minding his own business. He was visiting his uncle, Ray Seals, at the time one of the players on the Pittsburgh Steelers football team. The incident received some publicity; and put the Pittsburgh police in the national spotlight momentarily, but that was about it. Nothing much happened. In the meantime, a family in Syracuse had lost one its members.

CHAPTER FIFTEEN

WHO IS THE BOSS: PRETEEN YEARS WITHOUT FATHERS AS ROLE MODELS

The Davis household was like any other in a typical African-American neighborhood in a lot of ways. For one, it was headed by Genell Davis and she proved to be one tough woman, according to those who know her. That the Davis household was held down by a female is not unusual years ago as it is now. Back in the day, it was not uncommon for an African-American female to be the head of a household. It hasn't really changed much today. If anything, it has gotten worse. Statistics released by the government appear to indicate a worsening trend, and mostly it seems to affect African-American families more than others.

For reasons that have not been fully explained, many African-American men just don't stay around too long to help raise the kids they have with their wives and girlfriends

As stated earlier, the Davis household fit into that mold; the Davis children had to grow up pretty much without the active participation of a father. The Davis boys know now in retrospect that it was hard on their mother to take care of hardheaded boys like General with minimal input from their father. If it bothered Genell she didn't show it; at least, not to her kids. It was a responsibility she assumed and appeared to have taken care of it the best way she knew how.

Did she do a good job?

Of course, if you ask any of the Davis boys. Others might have a different opinion, but that's the way it was with the Davis boys. The fact that their father wasn't around didn't take anything away from the respect they had for their mother. As far as they are concerned, she played the role to the max, which was basically to take care of her kids.

Again, it was not unusual back then and now for fathers to be absent from the lives of their children for long periods of time. The father of the Davis offspring was typical in many ways. He did show up every now and then, and did it so often that it formed into a kind of a pattern. He would disappear for a while and then show back up, hang around for a while and then off again

It was hard getting used to the 'old man' not being around. After a while the Davis boys had no choice but get used to it and deal with it the best way they could. Life in the Bricks was brutal in every way you can think of. The Davis boys saw nothing but the real and hard life all around them; drugs, liquor, sex, and all the illegal things people do and go to jail for, both in the streets and at home.

Looking back, the Davis family, most of them now fully grown adults know they have no one to blame for what happened to them as they grew up. That was the way it was back then and they know their parents did the best they could under the circumstances.

Who do they blame for what happened to them that might have contributed to making them the kind of adults they became? Did the fact that they grew up in a mostly one parent home with their mother and brothers and a father who wasn't around impact negatively on them as a whole? Or being around brothers and a sister who, for all intents and purposes, had become nothing short of gangster types themselves at an early age? Or was it pre-destined that regardless they would have ended up the way they did, regardless?

This is what General has to say: "All I can say is I still don't know. As much as I have tried to analyze and to understand and put all the pieces together, I find myself unable to answer that all important question. And it's probably because I don't want to assume something that may not be true

I think it is for others to judge. All I can do is tell my story, describe the circumstances and let others make their assessment and decide for themselves what it was that pushed me into becoming such a notorious character at an early age."

CHAPTER SIXTEEN

EVERY PARENT'S NIGHTMARE; WHEN THEIR CHILDREN JOIN A GANG OR START 'HUSTLING'

Parents always think about it, but don't say it, fearing that talking about it might some how make it come true. But it is every parent's worst nightmare. We are talking about gangs and violence and death in the community that take away the lives of young ones, mostly young African-American teenagers or twenty something year old young men.

Statistics show that a huge percentage of young African-American men get killed mostly in the neighborhoods. So common are the neighborhood killings that it has almost become accepted as a fact of life: you're lucky if you're an African-American youth and live to be thirty.

According to the media, violence in most neighborhoods in American cities is mostly attributed to youth gangs. How valid that assumption is still being debated. It all depends on how one defines gangs. In some neighborhoods in many American cities, all it takes for law enforcement to designate a group as being a gang is for two or three young adults to be together, walking down the street, or standing in a corner or sitting in a car.

It gets even weirder when other factors are added by law enforcement to define gangs in neighborhoods. It has been suggested that if law enforcement spot two or more young adults wearing a T shirt of similar design and color, that is supposed to be one of the definitive signs of gang presence,

Our research into what constitutes a gang revealed something totally different. According to sociologists, the following is the definition of a gang.

Youth gangs are self-identified, organized groups of adolescents, banded together under common interests and a common leader in activities that typically are regarded as menacing to society or illegal. And it is not a new phenomenon either. Gangs, or their prototypes, have existed for hundreds of years in a number of cultures. Many scholars locate the emergence of the modern youth gang in the nineteenth century, during the shift from agrarian to industrial society. Most youth gangs arise among the urban poor, though not always. Although gangs participate in unlawful activities associated with controlling a territory or illegal enterprise, most of their pursuits remain purely social and within the law.

Historians have noted that gangs have been part of the social fabric for centuries and in different parts of the world. According to experts, youth groups have existed since at least the Middle Ages. Accounts from England in the fourteenth and fifteenth centuries describe criminal gangs that robbed, extorted, and raped. In France, England, and Germany, medieval juvenile groups known as abbeys of misrule participated in violent sports and fights against rival groups in honor of the abbeys from which they were recruited. Other youth groups rioted and intimidated deviant villagers, and were sanctioned by adults for enforcing the social order. In the seventeenth and eighteenth centuries, English gangs wore colored ribbons to mark their allegiances, battled rivals, and terrorized communities. In the American colonies, people complained about troublesome groups who caroused, fought, and stole, as well.

Although these earlier prototypical gangs possessed characteristics associated with the modern youth gang, quintessential urban street gangs only emerged in the nineteenth century. In the United States, the social and economic pressures associated with rapid industrialization, urbanization, and immigration gave rise to organized criminal gangs that thrived under these conditions. Gangs like the "Pug Uglies" and the "Dead Rabbits" conducted illegal activities in slums and recruited youths and adults. They were linked with the criminal underworld, saloons, and political machines. As new immigrants arrived and ethnic conflicts increased in the late 1800s, ethnic youth gangs battling for turf and status became more prevalent.

Urban reformers interpreted the gang phenomena as part of the depravity and degradation of city life. Alarmed by the tenacity and success of some of these organizations, they began to study the causes of gangs. Significantly, researchers focused on the role of juvenile DELINQUENCY in the development of adult criminal gangs. Partly as a result of these studies, many reformers throughout the late nineteenth and early twentieth centuries promoted child welfare services and education as a means of stemming gang activity and reestablishing social order.

Frederic M. Thrasher's work The Gang (1927) epitomized this new trend in the study of gangs. Thrasher located the roots of criminal groups not only in the miserable living conditions and economic disadvantages of the poor, but also in adolescent development. He proposed that gangs were a normal adaptation to slums and an extension of natural adolescent bonding. Young gang members entered into adult organizations only when social conditions remained inadequate and social mobility was unattainable. Influenced by Thrasher's study, public officials and experts throughout the 1920s and 1930s largely either dismissed juvenile gangs as adolescent play or elevated them to the level of adult organized crime, rather than recognizing them as menacing, independent entities of their own.

Youth gangs received heightened attention during World War II. In Europe, the disastrous upheaval of war caused a significant rise in delinquency. Acting out of necessity, juvenile gangs participated in the black market, prostitution, and theft. In the United States, the increase in youth gang activity was as much a product of Americans' new awareness of the problem as it was of true increases in numbers. Public officials and the media blamed wartime conditions, like disruptions in family life, for contributing to juvenile delinquency. At the same time, people became concerned with ethnic youth subcultures and fads, like the zoot-suit fashion. The style, and its connection to a series of race riots in 1943, created a situation in which minority youths began to band together into ethnic gangs for protection, and which also crystallized the public's conception of youth gang violence. By the end of the war, the combined awareness of the juvenile delinquency problem and of interethnic clashes solidified American's fears about youth gangs.

In the postwar period, American youth gangs were a major social dilemma on the streets and in the public consciousness. In the 1950s gangs were characterized by their ethnic and racial affiliations, their control of territory, and their greater use of violence against rivals. Law enforcement and social services targeted gangs for research, surveillance, and interventions, and the popular media portrayed youth gangs in movies like The Wild Ones. However, by the mid-1960s, adolescent gang activities slowed. Gang intervention programs and public policy did much to disrupt gangs. Scholars also suggest that political involvement in civil rights issues and the anti-war movement drew many youths away from gang participation, or redirected gang activities into militant groups like the Black Panthers. Moreover, the increased use of DRUGS such as heroin by gang members destroyed gang cohesion and created loose drug subcultures in its place.

Youth gangs resurfaced in the 1970s in response to the economic downturn in inner cities and to the growing drug culture. A number of returning veterans from Vietnam reorganized gangs and provided new leadership and experience. Though youth gangs actually fought against the prevailing drug culture at first, many juvenile gangs increasingly turned to drug trafficking for profit. By the 1980s, gangs were involved in more predatory crimes, and battled for control of illegal markets as well as turf. Gang activity was marked by brutal violence as gang members began to carry and use guns.

Modern juvenile gangs have been a problem around the world. Various youth gangs in Great Britain and Germany have emerged in response to ongoing class rivalries and rising immigrant populations, including rowdy and nationalist soccer hooligans and racist, violent skinheads. Studies in African youth gangs have also turned up groups like the skollie gangs of South Africa, who provide protection, support, and economic survival for their members. In Jamaica, posses recruit members living in extreme poverty, and commonly use violence and torture in their drug trafficking operations, and in Colombia, adolescent gangs protect territory and carry out murders for drug cartels.

Gangs have become refined in structure and modes of operation over the years. They have also expanded their reach. They are everywhere in all shapes, sizes and guises; in small rural communities as well as urban settings.

Response from law enforcement to the proliferation of gang activities in America has been just as intense. Gangs have been infiltrated and eliminated from coast to coast; gang leaders have been arrested and thrust into jail and given long sentences. Yet overall,.the danger that gangs pose remains strong, for the youth and their parents.

For the young adults and youth, there is the ever present possibility of either voluntarily becoming members of a gang, or being coerced, forced or intimidated into joining a gang. Regardless of how it happens, becoming a member of a gang increases the risk of violence and premature death for them.

For adults, it is the threat of losing an offspring as a result of gang related violence. For all of society, it gives meaning to what we describe as ' dead boys walking' when we talk about youth and young adults who get involved in gangs and other activities that set them up to be killed before their time.

CHAPTER SEVENTEEN

RICO LAWS: WHEN GOVERNMENT INTERVENTION ENDANGERS THE LIVES OF YOUNG BLACK MEN, HISPANICS AND YOUTH FROM OTHER RACES

A few years ago, Syracuse resident Lisa Blount decided to make as much noise as she possibly could to create awareness in her community about what the real deal was with a series of laws formulated by the federal government often referred to simply as RICO. She wanted the world to know that the RICO Laws had set in motion a process that would effectively destroy lives, ruin families, and ultimately reduce the African-American community into a wasteland populated by young women and men with no hope for the future.

Convinced that the RICO Laws were nothing but a systemic device put in place by the authorities to hunt down and eliminate young Black men, she dedicated herself to the task of raising public awareness about what she considered as the true nature and intent of the RICO Laws as they applied to the African American community, the danger they posed, the damage they had already done to the African-American community and the ultimate impact it would have. Unbeknownst to her, she was taking a stand against a law that was contributing to creating 'dead boys walking' in the community in which she lived.

Why Take the Risk?

What caused Lisa Blount to do what she did? Why would she feel so compelled to make statements, condemning federal laws that had wide ranging and powerful implications, the kind of action that would in all likelihood, bring her to the attention of the police and other law enforcement authorities such as the FBI? Why did she launch a public condemnation of the RICO Laws in Syracuse, a city with a police force known to be quick to close ranks on issues that have the potential to create problems for them, and just as fast to clamp down on people they think are talking too much or saying things they're not supposed to say?

According to Lisa Blount, she had a personal stake in the matter; her son had been taken into custody under the RICO Laws. And she was made to feel powerless, defenseless and weak after making all kinds of efforts to get him released. The law enforcement authorities couldn't give her any specific reasons to explain why her son had been taken into custody.

"All they said was they got him, under the RICO Laws."

At the risk of being labeled as just an angry mother, spewing forth rhetoric and smarting over a law that had been used to take her son away from her, she decided on a plan of action that would set her on a collision course with law enforcement; go public with her case and make as much noise as she possibly could. At that point, she didn't care about anything else except the fact that her son was behind bars and faced with the possibility of doing a long stint in prison. Worse yet, the case against her son was based on the RICO Laws, already being criticized in the media and the community in which she lived as biased against African-Americans.

Lisa Blount was far from naïve. For one, she knew she was not alone in feeling that way about the RICO Laws. The Syracuse African-American community was feeling the impact of the series of laws that were being enforced by law enforcement agencies that appeared to have targeted young Black men. All you had to do to break the RICO Laws, it seemed, was to have two or more young Black men wearing a T-shirt of the same color, hanging out together. As far as law enforcement was concerned, that was a gang. And that gave them enough reason to move in and arrest those young men. That was probable cause for an arrest, as far as law enforcement was concerned. The media had also published stories of police raids in neighborhoods that had been carried out under the guise of enforcing the RICO Laws.

She knew what the real deal was. She has lived in Syracuse long enough to know what you have to deal with when you tick the city police off. Coming out in the limelight and talking about something as politically charged as the RICO Laws meant one thing; the authorities would take notice, analyze what it's all about and make a decision. One of two things could happen in such cases: They would come down hard, under the guise of the law. They would pull you over and harass you in any number of ways. It had happened all too often in the past. According to Lisa Blount, that was precisely what happened to her son.

But that didn't deter her. If anything, it reinforced her conviction that she was doing the right thing.

Her encounter with the RICO Laws began as an up-close and personal tragedy, but her reaction was not just emotional; her decision to launch her drive was premised on the notion that the public seemed to be unaware that the RICO Laws had other motives besides the all too obvious effect of removing young Black males from society. Throwing young African American men in jail meant taking away and locking up young Black men in their prime who are fathers to young kids, husbands or boyfriends to young Black women; in effect creating the conditions that contribute to destroying the Black community.

"That's why you have much so called anti-social stuff going on. We talk about the rise of lesbianism among young black females. There are no young black men around with RICO Laws," she said.

Lisa Blount set her sights high. She aimed at accomplishing the ultimate in civic activism: bring her case all the way to Washington. Realizing that RICO is national in scope, and taking a cue from others who have preceded her, she decided to elevate her advocacy to the highest level by organizing what she described as a march on Washington.

She wrote on her page on FACEBOOK. "Who's brave enough to challenge RICO with me? It stops NOW!!! Calling all the brave troopers, and ride or die soldiers ready and willing to go all the way to Washington. This is a community, not a gang. Black or white. We all bleed red. Come out and help organize the March . . . ."

She is not your average African female. That's for sure. By taking that bold stand to talk about a powerful law legislated by the national government, it made her into a leader; she became a pioneer leading the community in a crusade to end a law she considered harmful to her community. Unbeknownst to her, she had set in motion, a movement that would contribute to helping many become aware of the fact that they were 'dead boys walking', as a result of a legal mandate from the federal government under the guise of a series of laws called the RICO Laws.

CHAPTER EIGHTEEN

HATE CRIMES: THE ROLE IT PLAYS IN THE CREATION AND PERPETUATION OF THE 'DEAD BOYS WALKING' SYNDROME

Recent events in Central New York appear to indicate that the incidence of hate crimes is on the increase. As one of the major cities in Central New York, Syracuse was thrust into the limelight when Moses Lateisha Cannon was killed on the westside. His crime; being different in the sense of being openly gay, and dressing in female clothing, making him a transgender.

Headlines in the media described his murder as a HATE CRIME. Recent media reports also appear to indicate that refugees on the Northside of Syracuse have been attacked, brutalized and harassed by others for no apparent reason other than the fact that they are different, speak a different language and wear different styles of clothing and attires.

Questions being asked range from why it is happening in Syracuse to when did it start, to what can be done about it to whether they are really hate crimes and what hate crimes are and how different they are from other violent crimes

That such crimes project a negative image of Syracuse is beyond question. That the murder of a city resident and everywhere else where it occurs is a tragic loss to a family is also beyond question. Equally distasteful is the notion that refugees live in fear in a country whose constitution guarantees freedom of movement and speech. The reality most Syracuse residents and people in other cities have to live with is that hate crime is real and had happened in their midst and potentially can happen again.

Can anything be done to stop the increase in hate crimes? That is the question being debated at the local, state and national levels and the debate continues.

As tragic as it was, the murder of Moses 'Tiesh' Cannon in November of 2008 on the west side of Syracuse, NY, immediately moved into center stage as the prime example of a hate crime. It occurred at a time when the local, statewide and national media had began to focus on a new theme in the legal realm labeled as hate crimes, being debated and defined as any crime committed against an individual who is perceived as different or abnormal and therefore an affront to others. Tiesh Cannon's murder would be the first hate crime in New York State to go on trial.

Suddenly, what begun as a homicide in a neighborhood on the West side of Syracuse was about to become a landmark case that would set a precedent for all other such cases to follow in all of New York state. Both the law enforcement authorities and the legal establishment knew and recognized the gravity of the case as well as the impact and ramifications the murder of Tiesh Cannon would have on state laws and federal laws if the case was handled as a hate crime.

The media hype continued, and got louder when the national media also began to focus on the subject of hate crimes, which also had the unintended result of legitimizing the claims and calls made by the Cannon family to prosecute Tiesh's murder as a hate crime.

Even those Syracuse residents who didn't know Teish Cannon or his family, his murder hit them hard, driving home the truth of what many community leaders had been talking about the past several years; the danger and death that stalk people, regardless of race, sex, and gender. Being at the wrong place at the wrong time can get you killed. For the youngsters, wearing the wrong colors can also get you in trouble with other gang members if you stray into their territory wearing 'enemy colors'

For a transgender, it was being at the wrong place at the wrong time.

CHAPTER NINETEEN

GROWING UP IN THE PROJECTS IN SYRACUSE

A dead boy walking in the context of what we are talking about in this book is anyone you know who is in their teens or mid-twenties or mid-thirties who has managed to survive being killed and is still walking the streets. Thus you should consider yourself lucky to have escaped early death, whether you want to admit it or not. And this applies to all youth and young adults no matter where you live this country or the world.

It is the truth. To have made it this far for most youth and young adults and other adults is nothing short of a miracle. It's scary to even think about it. It is quite possible that almost everyone you know in the city in which you live has had to deal with the death of a young member of their family as a result of violence. That is what we are writing about in this book. If anyone can be described as a 'dead boy walking' it can be none other than the youth and young adults of today. They come to mind when you hear that phrase; dead boy walking. Many live the kind of lifestyles that expose them to death at every turn.

Why? What makes them vulnerable?

We are not sure we know the answers to those questions in part because they are not as simple as they seem. They demand explanations that involve analysis of behavioral patterns as they impact the youth and young adults making choices in life at certain phases in their lives, all in a certain sociological context.

We leave that kind of analysis to the experts. That is their domain. They are equipped with the expertise and know how and have the ability to make a determination as to why many youth and young adults veer into a lifestyle that puts their lives in danger. This is General Davis' take on the issue: "I do know when I began behaving in ways that set me on the path to becoming a notorious gangster, as the media described me back in the day, the fascination I had for that lifestyle and who might have influenced me in that direction. I think it had a lot to do with who I had for a role model growing up in the projects in Syracuse and that was a big deal, to me, as it was to most of my peers, growing up.

My brothers were my role models. They filled a void created by the absence of a father whose presence might have made a difference. What difference it might have made I am not sure. There was no such presence, and its effect really didn't really register till later, probably because I was too young or the presence of my brothers provided a kind of substitute that to my young impressionable mind at the time, was good enough. That probably explains why I find it so easy to state that I had my brothers as my role models growing up.So what effect did that have on me? A whole lot. We had the bonding forged among us by virtue of being brothers, but there was a little more to it. Ours was a special bonding born out of a desire to uphold the reputation the brothers had built in the streets for being tough, wild and crazy. They were the type of dudes you didn't mess with. You knew what was coming if you crossed one of them.

I grew up in the projects at a time when this country was undergoing a serious transformation. The civil rights was at its peak and Syracuse was caught up in it right along with the rest of the country."

CHAPTER TWENTY

THE TOOKIE WILLIAMS STORY: THE PRIME EXAMPLE OF A 'DEAD BOY WALKING'

Stanley 'Tookie' Williams was executed by the authorities in California a few years ago. His execution made headlines all over the world for a number of reasons. For one, he was not your average prisoner; he was a prisoner with a national and global reputation that made him a popular figure even behind walls. He has been widely recognized as the founder and leader of the CRIPS, often described in the media as the most dangerous gang in the United States. The CRIPS was based mostly in the Los Angeles area where it began.

'Tookie' had achieved celebrity status by the time he was executed. He was famous and had become an international figure with support from people all over the globe. He was a real life big and bad dude. He looked, acted and lived like a big, bad dude. He was menacing and intimidating physique wise. His body bulged and bristled with muscles. He was known to carry guns he wasn't scared of using, and ready to brawl.

He was accused of various crimes. He denied committing those crimes, but the law enforcement authorities didn't believe him. They succeeded in putting him in jail with a death sentence as the ultimate punishment.

His execution hit many real hard, not so much for the cruelty of it in terms of a human life being taken, but for the fact that his story was a tragic reminder to many young men of what could have gone wrong with their own lives. The reaction from many across the country went ialong the following lines; why did he allow himself to be get caught in such a messy situation if he was that big and bad?

His life paralleled the lives of most 'dead boys walking' in many ways in the context of what we are talking about in this book.

Tookie Williams was your typical dead boy walking from the beginning of his life. He had sentenced himself to death early in life and didn't even know it. His lifestyle set him up to end the way he did. Support for 'Tookie' came from people protesting the death sentence for criminals. But it took on a life of its own and became something of a cause célèbre for many who viewed his death sentence as representing everything that is supposed to be wrong with the criminal justice system.

The name of Tyrone Hinds is known to many in the Syracuse African-American community and law enforcement authorities. Back in the day, he was one of the most popular young men in the city of Syracuse, possibly for all the wrong reasons. All kinds of rumors were circulated about him and what he was supposed to be doing. Whether the rumors were true or not, no one knew for sure. And didn't care really; what he did was his business, until he was busted, charged with a number of drug related crimes and locked up with a long prison sentence. What no one knew at the time was; he was a 'dead boy walking.'

There are many young men and women who are headed in the same direction like Hinds. These are young men and women who think it's cool to live the gangsta lifestyle. By the time they realize their mistake, it is too late; they're either dead or behind bars in a penitentiary doing time.

Did they kill an innocent man in the case of Tookie Williams as alleged by his supporters?

No one knows for sure whether Tookie Williams was guilty of the crimes he was charged with. He continued to profess his innocence until he took his last breath and was put to death. His innocence or guilt didn't matter much after he was killed. He had been silenced forever.

Did Tookie leave a legacy? Indeed he did. Again, possibly for all the wrong reasons, he remains highly admired and revered by the youth and young adults in this country and the world over. He was nominated for the Nobel Pace Prize for the role he played in negotiations to bring peace and harmony to neighborhoods as well as gangs.

Any act of youth related violence, be it a drive by shooting in the hood, or the murder of a young adult, reminds many African-Americans of how lucky they are to be alive today. Reading about the execution of Tookie Williams or the killing of Trayvon Martin shows how dangerous the streets are today, for both the innocent and those alleged to be engaged in criminal activity. Though he was executed, Tookie Williams was a typical 'dead boy walking' who paid the ultimate prize with his life when his death sentence was carried out. Trayvon Martin was also 'a dead boy walking' even though he was only going to the store to buy skittles for his father.

General Davis reflects on the parallels between him and Tookie Williams and writes: "The only difference between Tookie and I was he and his gang lived and operated in a big city on the West Coast and our gang, the Corleonnes operated in Syracuse, New York. Point is: it's just as likely for a city the size of Syracuse to become the turf of a gang as vicious as the Los Angeles Crips and Bloods. Ask any police, judge or sheriff about the kind of terror that was unleashed by the Corleones on Syracuse in the late seventies and you'll know what we're talking about.

That was back in the day. We were in our teens, and thought we were gangsters. It was supposed to be cool to belong to a gang back then as it is now. You had to belong to a gang, or pretend you did. It was the law of the streets back then as it is now, to repeat what I have just stated. The gangs ruled the streets and the neighborhoods. We could care less about the police, the sheriffs, the judges and the rest of the law enforcement establishment

We survived, and again, we can't even quite figure out how and why we did. Luck? Maybe. God's protection? Possibly. Sloppiness on the part of those who were supposed to stop us? More like it.

We attended funerals of some of our friends, and didn't know or stop to think that it could have been us. For all we knew, they were victims of their own bad luck. They allowed themselves to be killed. It was not our fault they were slow, and didn't pick up on what was going down whatever it was that got them killed. I have no idea how we survived and I don't think any of my boys had an inkling about the fact that we were all 'dead boys walking'."

CHAPTER TWENTY ONE

YOUTH VIOLENCE IN SYRACUSE, A MAJOR PROBLEM FOR CITY AUTHORITIES AND AFRICAN-AMERICAN COMMUNITIES

One of the most outrageous criminal acts in recent times in Syracuse was the shooting of a twenty month old baby, Rashad A. Walker Jr. The murder of the toddler occurred during a shooting on the Southside of Syracuse. According to media reports, both print and electronic, the baby was killed in a shooting in which the gunman targeted the wrong person. The father of the baby was the intended target of the shooting. The baby got hit by mistake.

The toddler's murder was not an isolated incident. Rather it was described as the culmination of series of a deadly game of hit and run shootings by members of Syracuse gangs. They were seeking revenge for acts carried out by rival gangs feuding over territory or other gang related activities involving mostly youth and young adults in Syracuse neighborhoods.

That deadly game of hit and run by gangs had destroyed another life in another shooting incident a few days earlier. On Nov 26, 2010, Kihary Blue was shot when the vehicle in which he was riding came under fire during a drive by shooting. The 19 year old college student was rushed to the hospital. He died as a result of the wounds he sustained in the shooting.

Reaction to the series of shootings was fast and furious. And it ranged from shock to anger to disgust to sadness. This was total insanity, said the media. The thought that a toddler, only twenty months old could get hit and be killed in a shooting incident struck many as the worst possible crime that could be committed, regardless of the circumstances in which it occurred.

The Syracuse media hyped it up, focusing on the victims, particularly, the toddler, a baby denied the right to live. So was the tragic end of Kihary Blue, described as a star athlete in high school and one who seemed to be on track to laying the foundation for a successful future. Of significance is the fact that the murders of the baby and Kihary Blue were seen and viewed not as isolated incidents, but in their wider implications in terms of their relation or linkage to gangs and gang related criminal activities in Syracuse neighborhoods. In other words, it addresses the point we are trying to make in this book; that gangs and the gangsta lifestyle can get you killed at an early age, no matter where you live.

Kihary belonged to a prominent African-American family in Syracuse. He was a member of the Blue family. His grandfather is Rev. Otis Blue, a leading businessman and a minister

As an outstanding athlete in high school, he had gained recognition on his own, made even more solid when he gained admission and went to college. He had everything going for him as they say, until that fateful day when it all came to a screeching halt. A hail of bullets fired from a passing car took his life.

It was not an accident, according to media reports, it was a planned hit, carried out by another young adult. His motive; revenge; he wanted to respond to a shooting that had occurred earlier. Problem was; Kihary had nothing to do with all the gangs and gang related activities described in the media reports. It was a tragic case of mistaken identity or being at the wrong place at the wrong time. However you want to look at it, it was the loss of a life that underscores the danger posed to the lives of innocent Syracuse residents as they walk or drive our streets, when gangs are involved.

Youth violence is nothing new to Syracuse. The city has the unenviable reputation of having one of the worst crime rates in the state of New York. Nothing to be proud, say city residents.

That his death was gang related is also nothing new. The media report such crimes all the time. Also nothing to be proud of. What made it more shocking is the brazen manner in which the entire episode was carried out.

Making it even more tragic were the victims involved; a college student who was not involved in any gangs or gang related activities and had nothing to do with gang revenge and a twenty month old baby who not only had nothing to do with it; just got caught in the cross fire and was killed before it had the chance to make it to his second year in life.

That it was gang related is what concerns many parents and law enforcement authorities in Syracuse and no doubt in any part of the country where youth violence has occurred. Something is wrong if kids can just go out and shoot at each other in broad daylight and go to court and talk about gangs seeking revenge

Something is wrong when a twenty month old baby can be killed as a result of such violence.

Again, the question is: what is being done about it? An arrest was made later and a lot of people were relieved that the perpetrator was arrested. He was prosecuted and made to face the full force of the law. He was finally penalized for the crime and committed to do a prison sentence for the crime.

The Syracuse media has focused considerable attention on the case by re-visiting it every year. The chief of police expressed his concern at the incidence of youth related violence in the city of Syracuse. Rev Otis Blue, the grandfather of the victim was interviewed by the media and agreed with the rest of the community that the arrest of the person responsible for shooting his grandson was a step in the right direction. He also added that it wouldn't bring his dead grandson back.

Can the streets be made any safer for the youth and young adults and more importantly the rest of the population in cities in this country? To what degree have the law enforcement authorities succeeded in combating gang activities to a point where we can all feel safe as we walk and drive our streets? These are some of the issues being raised in this book, basically to what degree have the law enforcement agencies succeeded in controlling youth violence in order to make the streets safe for city residents?

The jury is still out on that. No one knows for sure. But we must and will continue to seek answers from law enforcement, our politicians, our youth leaders and others who can and are involved in efforts to curb youth violence in cities all over the country.

CHAPTER TWENTY TWO

HELP FROM NON-PROFIT ORGANIZATIONS FOR YOUTH AND YOUNG ADULTS

He is nineteen years old and dropped out of high school in the eleventh grade. His life experiences, to date, have been nothing short of nightmarish. To hear him describe his constant brushes with the law, arrests and court appearances leaves you with the impression that this young man has either resigned himself to a life of criminality or has given up on doing anything positive with his life. Or perhaps, he has simply become captive to the criminal life. He is a typical modern day 'dead boy walking'

No matter how you look at it, one thing seems to stand out: he has lost control of his life even before he reached adulthood. And he knows it, too. What makes it even more frightening is his attitude: he sounds as though he has accepted the fact that his life is already a mess, and there is nothing much he can do about it.

He was released from prison about six months ago after serving a year's sentence for committing a felonious crime. He has since been looking for a job and can't seem to find one. When prospective employers find out about his record, they refuse to hire him. That is a dead boy walking and he doesn't even know it

He is fifteen years old, an outstanding high school student; he is pretty much on his own, he has to buy his own clothes, books, and take care of other things relative to his schooling.

She is eighteen years and is also pretty much on her own. With a mother who is suffering from cancer, with very limited income, she has had to survive by doing odd jobs after school to take care of her basic needs.

These are youth and young adults from varying backgrounds, and in different schools and situations. One thing is common between them: without help, they face an uncertain future and have to constantly deal with the risk of falling prey to temptations to engage in behavior that would get them in trouble with the law.

Remarkably enough they also share one characteristic; all of them claim to have sought help from a number of community based agencies in the city of Syracuse, with a specific need; to be provided with a job that would make it possible for them to make some money on their own. And none of them has found a job in part because no such programs exist that help the youth and young adults to find jobs that put money in their pockets; or if such agencies exist, they have terms and conditions that disqualify them. Last but not the least, the public and the youth in particular have no idea where they are or if any such programs exist, according to those we interviewed . . .

These are young men and women we talked to walking the streets of Syracuse today, who may not live too long because of the kind of lifestyle that they may be forced to live as a result of the circumstances in which they find themselves. If nothing happens to provide them with the kind of guidance, resources and support they need, they are likely to fall prey to pressure to do what may either end up sending them to jail or getting them killed That is the reality we have to live with.

Can the Youth Be Saved?

That the youth and young adults such as those mentioned above face challenges in their daily lives is beyond question; that some may succumb to temptations to drop out of school and hang out in the streets selling dope, and engaging in other criminal acts is also a fact. The question, though, is: can anything be done about it?

Why not? Sociologists cite studies that suggest various remedies. Cities like Syracuse are supposed to have facilities that run programs and activities that aim at complementing school curricula and which also provide recreational activities and programs designed to cater to the youth and young adults. For whatever reason, the existence of these facilities doesn't seem to have had an impact on the rising incidence of youth related violence. If anything, youth violence appears to be increasing. Concerned parents in the city and all over the country have voiced their concern, with the media continually hyping the issue. Yet the trend continues; youth violence is on the rise; drive by shootings involving youth and young adults have not abated; more young lives are being lost as a result of youth violence

New and Innovative Approach Needed

If the traditional approach of using community centers as recreational and educational outlets for the youth has been less than effective, it is time to try other ways, such as providing the youth with programs and activities that help them to find jobs or do things that provide financial rewards. One organization that has made a significant contribution to helping the youth and young adults to find jobs in the city of Syracuse is the Center for Community Alternatives. Its founder and staff have succeeded in creating a non profit organization that has relevance in terms of its impact on the delivery of services geared towards the youth, advocacy for and on behalf od the youth and young adults and putting in place programs that work.

Corporate America can and should step in and provide assistance to community based organizations that try to help youth and young adults to find jobs, pursue higher education, etc. In Syracuse, United Way founding has made it possible for such community based organizations as Dunbar Center and the Southwest Community Center to implement their programs and activities geared towards the youth and young adults. Lately, the funding has decreased or dried up entirely, leaving them with no choice but to cut back on their programs and activities. Nobody but the youth and young adults suffer when funding stops for community based organizations.

CHAPTER TWENTY THREE

DEAD BOYS WALKING IN JAIL OR IN THE STREETS: IT DOESN'T MAKE A DIFFERENCE

CNY VISION is a newspaper based in Syracuse, NY. It began publishing three years ago and has emerged within that period as the leading, most viable and most popular weekly newspaper that focuses on covering the African-American community. Kofi Quaye, co-author of this book was the first editor. Late last year it published an article written by Kofi Quaye in one of its editions. It was based on a response to a letter he received from one of his friends who was in jail. With the permission of the editor and publisher, we are reprinting the article.

It reads;

The other day I received a long letter from a friend in jail. By a long letter, I mean four pages of prose, meticulously written and in long hand, not computer generated as most letters are these days. And this came from someone who can't seem to be able to write under normal circumstances.

I was struck by a number of things, not the least of which was the fact that this particular person was able to pen such an elaborate missive to me in the first place. Secondly, it confirmed what has been said about people in confinement; they have nothing but time.

Writing wasn't his forte, he used to tell me, when I tried to encourage him to write for my newspaper. And I believed him. I knew him long enough to know the truth. Put a paper before him to write down his thoughts and he freezes. On the other hand, he is voluble in conversational exchanges. Anyone who meets him knows immediately that he is sharp, talks like someone with 'a good head on his shoulders', as the saying goes, is up on what's happening, and has all the other qualities we attribute to people who sound like they know what they are talking about, and have a certain degree of intelligence and awareness. Engage him in conversation and 'homeboy' has no problem stating his views and opinions in an intelligent and articulate manner

The tone of the letter was pensive, deliberative, and introspective. He wasn't proud of what has happened to him. Being incarcerated was the last thing he wanted, but he had no choice. It was the only option he had. He had been presented with a number of choices, but chose doing time in jail because it was the best. His rationale; probation was only a trap; he knew he wouldn't survive an extended period of probation. He was also penitent; and regretted the fact that he had created problems for himself and by implication, for his family. He would do the right things when he gets out, and make everyone proud of him

How in the world time in jail could be an option, I wondered. I asked and another friend with an extensive law enforcement background explained it to me. The gist of it was that he would have had to undergo a period of probation if he chose not to go to jail. And that is an option a lot of people don't want to deal with. It's hard to understand, but again, by the laws of the streets, it makes sense. With probation, you are free, but you will be sent back to jail with the slightest violation of the terms and conditions of your probation. And since most of the probation officers are white, and they have the power to make the decision, most African-American men don't like the idea of having their lives in the hands of white probation officers who have more love and respect for their dogs and cats and who have the power to send them to jail anytime they get ready.

He is in his early fifties, according to him, and has nothing to show for it. He has no children, no house, no apartment, no savings, no IRA. He lacks most of the basic items that most people own that make life convenient. He doesn't own a car, and of course, he has no job.

. I can understand how he feels now; certainly not unlike that of an animal in a cage. I have seen movies and read books about life in jail. Life in jail means losing one's freedom, becoming nothing more than a number in a system. It means you've hit the rock bottom and can't go any further, except the grave. I've sworn to myself that I'll do everything in my power to avoid going to jail. I still find it hard to believe that with some people in the streets, the rule is that you should feel less than a man, if you haven't done time in jail. This same friend in jail now used to laugh at me and called me a coward and a punk when I wouldn't join him when he felt the urge to confront the police in his drug or alcohol induced moments of macho valor. I know he's not laughing now.

Do I feel sorry for him? Indeed, I do, but the important question to me is; what happens to people like him who are either in jail serving time for crimes they committed or doing time for doing stupid things?

I learned a lot from him about the streets in a way I would never have had the chance if I chose to do what most Third World immigrants do; hang out with my own kind. He introduced me to another world where fast talking, fast moves, can earn you some money in deals that don't break any laws, but hurt only those who are slow. 'You slow, you blow' is the name of the game.

You haven't broken a law, they say, if you buy a television set worth $200 for $20 when you know the person selling it got from a 'booster' in exchange for drugs or got it out of his house in a moment of desperation because they need the money to buy drugs or liquor. The police might find probable cause to make an arrest if they catch you in the act of buying the merchandise in the streets, but they have no probable cause to stop you if you are driving your car down the street with a television set on the back seat or in the trunk.

The jails in our city, state and the country are full of such people who have broken the law in moments of desperation when all they wanted to do was to find a means to satisfy a habit. They didn't start out with a deliberate plan to commit a crime. But the law looks at it differently and prosecutes all with the same vigor, regardless of the motive. And when the unlucky ones such as my friend get busted, their lives are put on hold.

Many learn the big lesson life, which is to decide to do the right thing, rehabilitate themselves, drop the old bad habits and turn their lives around. Others just get recycled in the prison system.

I am not sure what the guy I am referring to will do when he gets out. All I can say is, it will be interesting to observe what he does with his life, hopefully something worth writing about.

Dead boy walking, he says it himself; he is damn near fifty years old and has no idea what he will do with his life. He has managed to escape the tragedy of an early and premature death, but his circumstances are in reality bad enough to make him a 'dead boy walking'

CHAPTER TWENTY FOUR

PRESENCE OF FOREIGN BORN YOUTH CONTRIBUTE TO DECREASE IN CRIMES? WHAT STOPS THEM FROM BECOMING THE NEXT YOUTH GANGS AND DEAD BOYS WALKING IN AMERICA?

The media, local, national and global deserve to be given credit for playing a key role in keeping communities informed on trends that indicate the latest developments in areas that impact their lives. Major newspapers such as the New York Times, Los Angeles Times, Chicago Tribune and others have established a firm tradition of keeping their readers informed by publishing articles, news items and editorials that aim at increasing awareness on the part of the general public on what's happening around them.

In Syracuse, the Post Standard in particular, the daily newspaper with the largest circulation in Central New York appears to have done an excellent job in the past in making the people in the community aware of what's going on around them.

It continues to do so by publishing articles every so often that contain data and relevant information that people use in their daily lives. It's also the kind of information needed by lawmakers, law enforcement and other governmental or non-governmental agencies that have committed themselves to providing services in various sectors. These include but are not limited to public safety, housing, transportation, youth services, and others too numerous to mention here.

An article published late last year in the Post Standard of Syracuse that was particularly striking and insightful in view of the conclusions made by experts and observers who were quoted. It was titled HOMICIDES ARE DOWN BUT VIOLENCE REMAINS, and it focused primarily on the fact that homicides have declined in the Syracuse metropolitan area. It came to our attention because it focused on youth violence. A number of factors were cited for contributing to the decline in homicides, among them, the fact that the presence of foreigners appears to have played a role.

According to the Post Standard, an influx of refugees in the last decade has brought at least 5,711 foreign-born residents to Syracuse. Most of the immigrants have shown a tendency to not commit crimes that lead to prison as often as native-born residents do. It also said that refugees have helped keep the city's population nearly stable as other residents moved out. The city lost 1,265 residents, or about nine-tenths of 1 percent, from 2000 to 2010. It quoted one observer as saying that most immigrants are hard working and law abiding.

There can be no doubt about the fact that this trend will be taken into serious consideration by all involved in any aspect of youth related work in the Syracuse metropolitan area. That youth violence is one of the major problems faced by the city is beyond question. That a lot of energy, time, and resources have been invested in an effort to combat youth violence is also well known. Drive-by shootings, stabbings, gang fights and other forms of violence involving mostly youth have given parents reason to be concerned about the safety of their kids.

From a sociological point of view, the fact that the presence of foreigners might have contributed to a decline in local homicides is significant in the wider context of how it can help in the overall task of keeping youth violence and homicides down, according to one Syracuse resident.

Another resident observed that there is a problem from the cultural standpoint with the youth of foreign descent that appears not to have been observed by the analysts. And that is the ever present tendency on the part of the majority of foreign born youth and young adults to try to assimilate into the mainstream by simulating the gangsta lifestyle. It happens as a result of being exposed to the latest trends in contemporary urban culture, which is dominated to a great degree by the hip-hop culture.

And the record of the hip-hop couture in terms of its relationship with morals leaves much to be desired, and that is stating it mildly. We are talking about youth and adults wearing pants hanging low down their waists, ear and nose rings, oversize T shirts and other trappings of the gangsta lifestyle. Isn't there a danger for these impressionable youngsters to gravitate towards that kind of lifestyle which in turn has the potential of influencing them to develop tendencies that may lead them astray? That is the question that comes to mind.

What will stop them from wanting to become the future gangstas from Africa in America? We alluded to child soldiers in another chapter. These are youth and young adults already exposed to extreme violence and potentially prone to returning to a life of violence if it presents itself as an alternative

Community groups cannot ignore the significance of these factors.

CHAPTER TWENTY FIVE

KEEP THE YOUTH CENTERS OPEN TO COMBAT YOUTH VIOLENCE

Lately, the Spanish Action League of Syracuse has faced huge problems that threaten its very existence, stemming mostly from lack of finding. Another organization, the Southside Business Center, initiated by a community leader and politician called Mike Atkins came to an abrupt end, two years after it was started, in spite of efforts by many in the community to save it. They had put considerable energy, time and effort into creating and running it. Besides, it provided an important service to the community. They didn't prevail. The center closed to the dismay of many.

The Dunbar Center on State Street, the oldest community center on the Southside of Syracuse teeters on the verge of annihilation: at least that was the impression created by media reports. The oldest community center on the Southside of Syracuse, the Dunbar Center has fallen on hard times and can't seem to be able to get the assistance it needs to continue to function effectively. Regardless of efforts by the leaders and members of the community, and appeals for help to city and corporate funding sources, no progress appears to have been made to stop the threat of closure. Lack of funding has forced the management to curtail, or scale down many of the services it has provided for decades. It has survived so far, but barely, sustained mostly by the gallant efforts of volunteers and staff who are hanging in there, hoping for a miracle to happen.

It's been bad news lately for non-profit organizations in the Syracuse metropolitan area and indeed the entire country. It has been particularly bad for community based non profit organizations located in the inner city and running programs and activities benefiting minorities. Well known and long standing organizations in Central New York such as the Spanish Action League and the Dunbar Center as well as lesser known upstarts such as the Mysteek Foundation and the Determination Center of CNY appear to face the same problem: lack or absence of funding. Sources of funding have dried up or disappeared altogether, making it almost impossible for the non-profit organizations to continue with their work on behalf of the targeted population to whom they provide service

It comes as no surprise if you haven't heard about the Determination Center of CNY or Mysteek Foundation or Africa Bound. They have not been in the news for receiving a grant to undertake projects with grandiose titles like other non-profits you've read about in the newspapers or whose programs and activities have been shown on television

Essentially, there is not much difference between the popular non-profits and the lesser known non-profits in terms of how they are constituted, or the intent and motive that create them. They were all set up by individuals and or groups of individuals driven by altruism and the conviction that they have the capacity and ability to contribute to their community and can do so using the non-profit model.

Furthermore, they have to file the same documents, answer the same questions, provide similar information to qualify to be granted tax exempt status as NGO'S. So the question becomes; why do some get the funds, get much publicity, seem to be accomplishing the goals they set for themselves while others barely survive, kind of waddle along or just go out of business altogether?

A number of characteristics stand out that indicate trends in the operation of non-profits in terms of the factors that seem to make or break them. Available evidence suggests that the majority of the organizations that face serious problems are based in communities populated by African-Americans and Hispanics. Number two: they were initiated, and are mostly run by minorities. Does it mean then that lack or absence of funding is more of a problem for non-profits in the minority communities?

The media has provided answers already; sort of. Considerable coverage has been given to the problems faced by the non profits across the board; the state has cut back on funding; fund granting agencies have less to give; money is tight every where. And in some instances, the senior staff of the community centers have a record of management that has been less than ideal.

In Syracuse, a new organization called The Mary Nelson Center is now located in the same building that housed a business center that was closed and is playing an important role in providing after school programs and other activities geared towards helping kids stay in school. In one sense, the closing of the business center was a loss, but not altogether, since it has been replaced. But other community based organizations such as the Dunbar Center, continue to face funding problems, no matter how hard they try. Sources of funding have simply dried up.

One thing is for sure; the non-profits in the minority communities all over the country have no option but make a real effort at organizing and relying on resources and support from within their own communities, manage their affairs more effectively and avoid some of the scandalous behaviors often attributed to them.

CHAPTER TWENTY SIX

AM I A DEAD BOY WALKING?

At this point, we want to believe that you know all about the dead boys walking syndrome. The preceding chapters have discussed what it means, who fit into that category and what happens to them. You have learned enough to be able to ask and answer the question above. Am I a dead boy walking?

The same question applies regardless of whether you are an older person or not, or live in a small or a big city. Regardless of the circumstances in which you find yourself, you have to ask yourself this all important question. Asking yourself that question will force you to face the reality in your life. And it all boils down to one thing; did you do the right thing in the past and or are you doing the right thing now?

Am I a dead boy walking? To truly answer the question, you have to look at your life in a way you have never done before and be prepared to be true to yourself.

You begin by asking the big question; what is happening with your life right now, considering how your life is situated today, in terms of what you are doing, with whom, when and how. If it looks like or seems like It's all about the streets for you; if the streets have become a home away from home; and have become part of your life in a way you never thought would have been possible, you are close to or already a 'dead boy walking'.

In light of what you do with your life, you have to ask yourself again and again: Will I live to be twenty two, twenty five, thirty years, forty years, fifty or sixty years old? You probably don't know all the answers or don't even care. If the lifestyle you lead is one that puts your life at risk in any shape or form, you are a 'dead boy walking' and need to do something about it. That's all there is to it.

If you feel that way about yourself, that you are only living from day to day, you're nothing less than what this book is about; a dead boy walking. It's not different from having a death wish; your life is headed that way if you continue with that lifestyle, you can get killed.

Eugene Kimbrough of Syracuse knows this kind of life only too well; he has been in jail most of his life. He is in his fifties and currently doing time for a crime he committed that was reported in the local newspapers. He is a 'dead boy walking' and has been one all his life, it seems. And as sad at it may sound, there are many like him, walking the streets or languishing in jails. Their lives have been shattered dreams. They are all victims of the dead boys walking syndrome.

CHAPTER TWENTY SEVEN

IS IT COOL TO BELONG TO A GANG?

The question most youth and young adults confront at some point in their lives is whether or not to join a gang. It's almost impossible to avoid and an inevitable challenge. Sooner or later, most youth and young adults have to confront that reality and deal with it and there are only two ways to deal with it; join or don't join.

That is one decision that most parents have no input. They don't even know about it when their kids get to that point in their lives where they have to make a decision to join a gang or face the consequences if they don't. In most instances, most kids will not discuss their decision with their parents. It's a decision they basically make on their own with no advice from an adult.

Quite often they have no choice. In some neighborhoods, it has become part of the fabric of life. And some kids find themselves already in some kind of gang just for living and interacting with other neighborhood kids in the area in which they live.

It becomes dangerous when the kids start openly identifying themselves as belonging to a gang. That focuses attention on them not just from neighborhood residents, but from the police and other law enforcement who look for the slightest signs of gang activity as an excuse or reason to move in and make arrests or harass.

That is one of the reasons why we say it's not cool to join a gang, for the simple reason that it is one of the major causes of the dead boys waling syndrome. Why would we say joining a gang is not cool? Because we know people who 'have been there, done that and know all about it' and have nothing to show for it but broken lives and shattered dreams.

For one, it is one way of setting oneself up to be killed at an early age. Stanley Tookie Williams paid the ultimate prize for belonging to a gang; he was executed. Thousands of lives have been lost prematurely all over world as a result of gang related violence.

It becomes dangerous when the kids start openly identifying themselves as belonging to a gang. These are some of the telltale signs to look out for. It has been reported that gangs tend to be identified by the attire they wear, the language they communicate with and their behavior which usually borders on the unethical, if not outright lawless. Both parents and youth and young adults have to watch out for these early warning signs of gang related activities.

All said and done, it's not cool to belong to a gang, for the simple reason that it is one of the major causes of the dead boys walking syndrome. That's why we say joining a gang is not cool. It is one way of setting oneself up to be killed at an early age.

CHAPTER TWENTY EIGHT

AFRICAN-AMERICAN YOUTH: AN ENDANGERED SPECIES AND DEAD BOYS WALKING: TRAYVON MARTIN, A PRIME EXAMPLE

In an interview on Piers Morgan on CNN in March 2012, Chaka Khan made a bold statement. She stated that African-American youth of today are an endangered species and stand in constant danger of being gunned down or killed or maimed no matter what they do or where they live. She was commenting on the ramifications of the Trayvon Martin tragedy.

The Trayvon Martin tragedy has emerged as one of the most controversial cases of a death resulting from a confrontation between an African-American and a white American in recent years. Teenage Trayvon Martin was shot and killed by George Zimmerman in Sanford, Florida. For reasons not fully explained by the law enforcement authorities, the incident appeared to have been kept out of public notice and not given the kind of attention such serious cases demand. To make matters worse, the perpetrator of the crime remained free. Law enforcement cited a law in Florida that justifies the use of deadly force by people who find themselves in situations where they have to defend themselves Zimmerman claimed he acted in self defense. He was also acting in his capacity as a member of the neighborhood watch.

The parents of Trayvon Martin, concluded otherwise. They accused Zimmerman of killing their son in cold blood. They also accused the Sanford police of inaction and collusion and demanded that the perpetrator be charged with murder and be made to face prosecution and given the appropriate punishment for murdering their son

Nothing much happened until the news of the incident went viral on the Internet. The Internet helped to circulate it to the rest of the world and contributed significantly to making it the hottest news on the airwaves the second half of the month of March 2012.

Chaka Khan was certainly not the first to make a statement to the effect that the African-American youth and young adults of today are an endangered species. That sentiment has been articulated by many over the years. But it has somehow been viewed as race based rhetoric used by alarmists seeking to shock the public with such statements. It has been repeated by many, especially in circumstances where the lives of young African-American are lost to violence

Chaka Khan was serious when she articulated that notion, and in the wake of the Trayvon Martin tragedy, it had the ugly ring of truth that moment because of the circumstances surrounding the death of Trayvon Martin. The nation was dealing with a prime example of a death of an African-American youth whose death had occurred in mysterious circumstances, to say the least. George Zimmerman, the accused killer claiming self defense was still free, walking the streets, not charged with any crime.

Again, the world knows what happened when the news of the tragedy was finally picked up and hyped in the media. It galvanized the leaders of the African-American communities into action. So did the general population of African-Americans all over the country. Incensed at what appeared to be insensitivity on the part of law enforcement and sensing that the root causes may lie in the fact that the perpetrator was white, they joined forces and descended on the town of Sanford in their multitudes, to demonstrate and demand that justice be done.

In a way, the murder of Trayvon Martin, as tragic as it was, demonstrates the truth in what Chaka Khan and others have been saying for the longest; that the African-American youth and young adults of today are an endangered species. That is even made more ominous by the thought that it can happen anywhere and the possibility that law enforcement will act in pretty much the same way no matter what or where it happens in the United States.

So the question is; what can we do to prevent such incidents from occurring in our communities? Can anyone really do anything to stop such an incident from taking place in their community?

President Barack Obama commented on the incident and shed light on the ramifications of such a tragedy on parents, the African-American community and the entire nation. He made the following statement. "I have to be careful about my statements to make sure we're not impairing any investigation that's taking place right now. But this is obviously a tragedy. I can only imagine what these parents are going through . . . And when I think about this boy, I think about my own kids. And I think every parent in America should be able to understand why it is absolutely imperative that we investigate every impact of this and that everybody pulls together-federal, state, and local—to figure out how exactly this tragedy happened. I think all of us have to do some soul searching to figure out how does something like this happen. And that means that examine the laws and the contest for what happened as well as the specifics of the incident. But my main message is to the parents of Trayvon Martin. If I had a son he'll look like Trayvon Martin. And I think they are right to expect that all of us as Americans are going to take this with the seriousness it deserves, and that we are going to get to the bottom of exactly what happened."

The days of bling seem to be gone when the youth and young adults blatantly showed off their macho and gangsta tendencies in ways that offended and angered many, but that has not lessened the danger posed to African-American youth.

It has also been suggested that the real danger to the youth and young adults of America comes not so much from whites or people of other races than from other African-American youth and young adults.

And that is true in most cases. More youth and young adults are gunned down or killed by African-American youth and young adults. A tragedy such as that of Trayvon Martin highlights the danger posed as a whole by society at large.

The role played by what has been described as Black on Black crime cannot be overlooked. It doesn't get hyped in the media, but is just as vicious and tragic when they occur. Can anything be done about it? The answer is yes. It just doesn't make sense to kill anyone for whatever reason.

ADVERTISEMENT